It's always been You

L.L. Diamond

It's Always Been You
By L.L. Diamond

ISBN-13: 978-1-7342783-1-6

Facebook: https://www.facebook.com/LLDiamond
Instagram: @l.l.diamond
Twitter: @LLDiamond2
Blog: http://lldiamondwrites.com/
Austen Variations: http://austenvariations.com/

Other works by L.L. Diamond include:

Rain and Retribution
A Matter of Chance
An Unwavering Trust
The Earl's Conquest
Particular Intentions
Particular Attachments
Unwrapping Mr. Darcy
It's Always Been You
It's Always Been Us
It's Always Been You and Me

To those who have and will touch my life.
Every interaction, no matter how small, is a source of
inspiration.

I thank my family, friends, and my readers for the inspiration
you've freely given me.

Part 1

Chapter 1

When I first laid eyes on the expanse of pristine white beach, I slid off my sandals, stepped down from the dock to the water's edge, and gave in to the urge to squish the damp sand between my toes. The warmth of the sun magically prickled my skin as I took a deep breath, inhaling the air kissed with the heavy, salt scent of the sea while brilliant aquamarine water stretched forever until it darkened when it met the cloudless azure-colored sky. A slight breeze wafted in from the sea along with the occasional whitecap that broke along the sand. I still couldn't believe I stood there absorbing every last breathtaking bit. I'd saved up for years for this vacation, and I was finally here. Two weeks! Two weeks to snorkel, lay out on the beach, or maybe scuba dive if I felt like it. Whatever I wanted. I was servant to no one's whims but my own.

My plane had landed mid-afternoon, so it was already too late to plan anything for today, but I would definitely have to decide what to do tomorrow. I'd never traveled on my own before but why should being alone be an issue? I wouldn't have to check with someone else before I made plans, and I wouldn't disappoint or frustrate someone if I wanted to be lazy and relax in my villa with room service and a chick flick—not that I had any intention of doing so. At least, not yet.

"Miss Barrett?" I tore my eyes away from the picturesque view in front of me to the uniformed porter ambling down the dock. "Your bags are in your villa, number ten, just down on the left. Are you sure you don't need me to introduce you to the amenities we offer?"

I shook my head. "No, thank you. I'm certain I can figure it all out on my own. I am interested in snorkeling tomorrow. Could you recommend a guide perhaps? Someone who knows the best places and can take me there."

"You're welcome to snorkel off the deck of your villa, but the resort also offers tours. Your villa has a portfolio with all of our packages on the desk near the phone. Be sure to call as soon as you decide. You never know when the tours will fill quickly."

I lifted one side of my lips. "Of course, I will. I suppose I would've known about the portfolio if I'd let you show me around. I apologize."

"No worries, miss. If you require anything further, feel free to call our concierge desk. One of our staff will be happy to assist you."

"Thank you." I opened the small purse hanging at my side and pulled out a tip, which the young man accepted with a thank you before heading back toward the huge hut-like building that housed the lobby, the restaurants, and probably some sort of conference center.

A warm breeze rippled through the palms behind me, blowing the long curls back from my face and pressing my gauzy white skirt against my legs. The resort was paradise—no fussy clients, no work, no family, no one to please but myself.

My sister Jena was right. I did need this. The biggest question now was what to do first?

That wasn't a difficult question to answer. A shower to wash the stale airplane smell from my hair and skin was a must! By the time I dressed, the different restaurants at the resort would be open for dinner. I'd need to call and book a reservation, not to mention schedule that snorkeling tour for the earliest slot available tomorrow.

My footsteps made a steady cadence down the wooden planking of the dock until I reached my villa on the left, but before I could open the door, a loud voice from one of the huts nearby almost made me jump out of my skin.

"No, I just arrived yesterday. I have no intention of leaving so soon." I lifted my eyebrows. Whoever he was, his voice held a low tone that did not sound happy.

"No, I will not. I have some things I need to take care of and this is as good a place as any. I'll see you when I return."

I took another step but stopped when the voice continued, "How would you come here? You don't even know where I am. Really, this is ludicrous. I asked for some time, and I intend to take it. Please don't call me again. I'll contact you when I'm ready to talk. Goodbye."

With a quick peek, I checked to see if anyone noticed me standing there. What if he came out of his villa and found me listening? Not that I could avoid overhearing his conversation with how loud he was speaking, but it had still been rude to listen. I should've gone inside and booked that tour for tomorrow instead of being unbearably nosy. Before someone could catch me up to no good, I hurried inside. I had no intention of getting on that man's bad side! Whoever he was.

When I stepped back onto the dock a few hours later, the sky had morphed from that azure blue to an amazing sunset, awash with vibrant hues of red, orange, and purple and the water had become darker with the setting sun, looking more an inky black than the brilliant topaz of earlier. It was beautiful.

I had no desire to rush, so I didn't walk quickly. Instead, I took my time almost meandering down the walkway toward the main building of the resort, simply enjoying the sound of the waves breaking along the dock and the calls of a seagull from somewhere further down the beachfront. A gentle breeze still blew off the water, blowing my billowy sundress out from my legs. Unlike when I arrived, I stuck to the deck this time so I didn't get sand in my favorite strappy sandals. I doubted the restaurant would appreciate it if I showed up barefoot—even if they didn't have a sign that said, "No shirt, no shoes, no service," it was still tacky.

The resort boasted a myriad of places to eat, but since it was my first evening, I planned on celebrating. I was on vacation, the one I'd dreamed of forever. Tonight was definitely a special occasion. I'd perused all the choices back in my room and chose a grill called Salt Water. Fine dining and an ocean view to enjoy while I ate—it sounded perfect.

As I approached the maître d' podium, a man bumped my shoulder as he hurried around me. "Table for one, please." I stopped and stared. What a prick!

The host glanced at me then back to him. "Do you have a reservation, sir?"

"No, I was tied up with business most of the day," the man said with a huff as he shifted on his feet. "I didn't get a chance to call."

The maître d' shook his head. "I'm sorry, sir, but we're booked. Might I suggest the Thai restaurant? I know they have free tables this evening." The host's eyes returned to me. "Do you have a reservation, miss?"

With a careful step forward, I nodded. "Yes, Ellie Barrett." I sneaked a peek at the man beside me. His eyes flickered to me before they returned to the host, whose finger trailed along the iPad he held tilted toward him.

"Ah, yes." The host picked up a menu and held out his arm. "If you'll follow me."

That was when the man turned, his crystal blue eyes meeting mine, making me pause and swallow a gasp. Were those natural? I'd never seen a shade that clear and vibrant. I'd be willing to bet they'd probably match the shade of the water if it wasn't so dark outside. I started to step past him, but something stopped me. Who knew what that something was, but I simply couldn't leave him standing there. "Would you care to join me for dinner?"

His eyebrows drew down a little in the middle. "You wouldn't mind?"

"I'm dining alone, and I'm sure the table will be large enough for two. If you don't mind sharing with a stranger, I don't mind either."

I almost startled at how his face transformed when a small smile cracked the stern façade. I clenched my hands at my sides to keep from fanning myself. Good Lord, he was good looking! Two dimples peeked from his cheeks, his eyes crinkled a little at the edges, and most women would kill for those eyelashes. They were the longest I'd ever seen on a man. I even had eyelash envy! With his sculpted face, striking eyes, and dark brown hair, very few women would have had a dry chin in his presence.

"Thank you," he said. "I'd be happy to join you."

The maître d' took one more menu from the stack and showed us to a table along the edge of the decking. I stopped and stared at the unencumbered view of the sand and sea until the maître d' pulled out my chair and saw us seated and looking over the evening's selections before hurrying away.

"Thank you again for sharing your table."

I looked up from my menu and relaxed back into my seat. "I'm happy to do it. As I said, it's just me, I have the room, and I don't mind the company."

He held his hand over the table. "William."

"Ellie," I said. I feigned shifting as I leaned forward so I could press my damp palm against the cushion of the chair. I would not shake his hand with sweaty palms! "It's nice to meet you."

"Nice to meet you too." He cleared his throat while he scratched the back of his neck. "I'm sorry for pushing ahead of you back there. It's really nice of you to invite me to share your table considering how rude I was."

"Do you always shove women out of the way when you're hungry? Should I keep a look out for you in the future? Take a peek over my shoulder before I serve myself from the breakfast buffet?"

His deep chuckle traveled to the pit of my stomach where it caused a sudden flip. "Perhaps someone else might need to keep an eye out, but I'll make sure I don't bowl you over again. I promise."

"I appreciate that," I said with a laugh as I picked up the wine menu. "Would you like to share a bottle of wine? I thought I'd order some Prosecco."

He lifted his eyebrows. "Are you celebrating?"

"Actually, yes. I've been saving up for this trip, and I'm finally here. I think it's a good reason to break open some bubbly."

"How long have you been planning this?"

"Since I graduated college. My sister, my best friend, and I started our own company, and when we started making a profit, I began to put a certain amount away from my earnings every month—so about six years. We've also been saving up for a better office space so it's taken a little longer than it would otherwise."

He opened his mouth to respond, but the waiter appeared seemingly from nowhere, took our drink order, and bustled off.

William leaned back in his chair. "What exactly do you do?"

Every muscle in my back stiffened. Most men liked to poke fun at my job. I was on vacation. I didn't want to spend my first evening defending my profession. "I'm a wedding planner."

"Really?" he said, leaning forward and resting his forearms on the table. "I've always wondered what type of degree someone needed to do that."

"You don't necessarily need a degree, but business, design, and public affairs are typically helpful. I studied design, my sister studied communications, and Charlie double-majored in business and finance."

"I take it she handles the bottom line," he said with a crooked grin.

"Pretty much. So, what is it you do?" He didn't make a joke, comment that I planned occasions for lazy people or bash romance . . . yet. It was still a good time to change the subject, just in case.

The waiter returned and set to work serving our Prosecco. William glanced up at the movement but quickly returned to me.

"I own a construction company. We deal in new builds, custom floor plans, and such. The company originally belonged to my father. I earned my degree in architecture and took over when he wished to retire." He sipped the wine set in front of him and gave a nod for the server to continue.

I snuck a peek at his left hand. I couldn't help it! He was completely out of my league, but a girl could dream, couldn't she? No ring and no tan line from one either, so he was unmarried. Why would someone who looked like that and was obviously successful still be single? "Are you here on your own as well?" It was a reasonable question. Hopefully, I didn't sound like I was fishing for information on a potential girlfriend or even boyfriend somewhere out there.

"No, I needed to get away. My father's filling in for me while I take some time for myself. He insisted." He gave a light laugh. "I saw no reason to argue with him."

"I know what you mean." The bubbles from my wine tickled my tongue as I swallowed.

"So, let me ask you a very important question." He gave me a sidelong glance with a slight upturn of his lips. It was all I could do to keep my knees from knocking together. "What do you think of books?"

I leaned against the arm of my chair and tilted my head. "That's a serious question. I actually read more than I watch television."

"But what do you prefer to read?" He relaxed and crossed his arms over his chest. "Do you read about sparkly vampires, thrillers, boy wizards, or romantic earls in whatever completely non-romantic era?"

A burst of a laugh escaped before I could prevent it. "I've never read anything with sparkly vampires, I've read a few thrillers, I love to read about boy wizards and their quests, and I will sometimes read about romantic earls. If it's well-written, I'll read it."

"I can't tell you how relieved I am you don't care for sparkly vampires."

I lifted my eyebrow. Yes, I was flirting and I didn't care. What did I have to lose? "And what do you read, sir? Biographies, legal dramas, or maybe *you* enjoy those romantic earls."

He grinned and shook his head. "I've never read a story with an earl or even a viscount."

The waiter returned for our food order, but as soon as he was gone, we picked up where we left off. William wasn't just easy on the eyes, but he was also easy to talk to. He read a lot and it definitely showed. Dinner with him proved to be more interesting than most of the dates I'd had in the last five years. Yes, I possessed a sad and pathetic love life. The best prospect

I'd had in a long time was a stranger I'd met in the middle of paradise and probably would never see again. Yet, something about him tugged at me—not literally, of course. I couldn't explain it another way if I tried.

When the meal came, the food was cooked to perfection, and we ordered another bottle of wine. Even with the interruptions, our conversation never faltered once.

When the server brought the bill, I reached for it, but before I could so much as lay a finger on the edge, William scooped it up and signed it.

"How much do I owe you?" I edged forward in an attempt to see what was written, but he curled the paper toward him. I'd thought we'd split the tab. As much as I could wish it was, tonight wasn't a date.

He smiled and shook his head. "It's on me. You don't know how much I appreciate your offer to share the table, and I can't tell you how much I enjoyed having company for dinner. Thank you."

"I had a great time, too, but I never expected you to pay."

He held up the tray, which the server grabbed as he passed. "It's done. Maybe we'll be able to eat together again during our trip. You can pay then."

"I'll hold you to it."

"Great!" He stretched his arms over his head. "I would love to stay and talk some more, but I'm still a bit jet-lagged from yesterday."

If I was being honest, today's travel was beginning to wear on me as well. The conversation had been amazing, but eventually, I would fall asleep on the table if we stayed so I followed his lead and stood. "I know what you mean. It took a couple of long plane rides to get here. Between that and the wine, I'm sure I could fall asleep in a matter of seconds."

We didn't talk as we strolled from the restaurant and down the dock in the direction of the villas, but the silence wasn't awkward or uncomfortable. Instead, it was relaxed and oddly like it was supposed to be that way. He stood tall while he walked casually with his hands in the pockets of his pants. We both gazed out over the water where the moon hung low at the horizon.

When I started to veer onto the path to my villa, I pointed. "I'm this way."

He peered down the walkway with his brow furrowed. "Really? So am I."

We turned and walked steadily until we reached my door. I faced him and sort of pointed toward my suite. "This is me." At his nod, I held up my hand in a wave, instantly wanting the water under the dock to suck me in. I must've looked ridiculous. "Thank you for a lovely evening."

He nodded and glanced down to his feet then back at me. "Good night, Ellie."

I smiled and backed inside while I opened the door behind me. "Good night."

Chapter 2

I grabbed the blue crochet bag Jena made me from the desk. One last dig through confirmed I had a towel, sunblock, and a spare set of sunglasses—just in case! I was supposed to meet the tour at the dock in front of the resort. I glanced at the clock by the bed. If I hurried, I would barely make it.

I rushed as quickly as my flip flop clad feet could move along the pier without somehow falling ungracefully on my face. When I made it to the boat, a man was untying it from the dock. "Ellie Barrett?" I called to the man on board with the clipboard. He nodded and held out his hand to help me step to the deck.

"You didn't mention you were snorkeling today?"

I ungracefully pivoted around at the deep, newly familiar voice to find William smiling. "You didn't mention it either." I know I said it before, but wow, he was handsome! Something inside me fluttered whenever I looked at him, and I really had to work not to make an idiot of myself.

He shrugged, his arms out as though he meant to catch me if I fell from my klutzy pivot. "I made the reservation on a whim this morning." At his low chuckle, I swear I held my breath. "I had a hard time deciding between everything there is to offer."

"I—" Before I could speak, the boat chugged to life and began to move away from the pier.

He stepped toward the benches along the railing. "We should sit. When he clears the no wake zone, we'll probably start moving pretty fast."

"Do you know where we're going?"

"No, but the concierge said the guide knows the best spots around the resort."

I looked at the crystal-clear water and the spattering of puffy clouds in the sky. "It's beautiful here, isn't it?"

"Very," he said.

His presence beside me caused a hum in my body that I couldn't ignore, but I didn't want to miss the view. An occasional gull soared overhead, coasting along the air currents, and the white sand bottom of the ocean passed under us until the boat picked up its pace as we began cruising further out in the direction of a smaller island in the distance. The wind whipped around me, pressing my tie-dye coverup to my body and making the tendrils of hair that escaped my loose braid whip around in my face. A slight mist from the boat's wake cooled my skin.

When the guide stopped the boat, he gave a quick announcement of our location and instructions in the event of an emergency before releasing the eight of us on board to enter the water to explore.

I stood, removed my wrap, and pulled a rash guard out of my bag to put on over my bikini top. I burned way too easily and had no intention of asking a stranger to apply sunblock to my back, though I might consider allowing William if the idea didn't make me so jittery.

When I turned back to face him, the man in question cleared his throat. Had William been watching me? I couldn't help but get a certain satisfaction if he had. His cheeks held a slight tinge of red, but that could also be because of how balmy it was already, couldn't it? He held up a bottle. "Do you need sunscreen?"

What I could reach was already a bit slick with the spray I'd used earlier. "No, thanks. I put some on before I left."

Nodding, he began to smear lotion over his arms as the guide handed me a mask and snorkel and had me select my size fins from a bucket. I thanked him and smiled at William. "I guess I'll see you out there." Something in me wanted to wait until he was ready to go, but how needy and pathetic would that make me? I couldn't stand there and stare at him with my tongue lolling out of my mouth like a drooling dog. I could do this! I would do this—even if his muscles all shifted deliciously when he moved. Stop it, Ellie! I was not going to make a fool of myself. I wasn't.

By the time I made it to the platform at the rear of the boat, the others on the tour were already in the water and swimming in different directions. I sat on the edge and dipped my legs into the warm water, the salt slightly stinging my newly shaven legs.

"Do you have a swimming partner?"

The guide stood over me when I peered up, using my hand to shield my eyes from the blinding angle of the sun. "No. Is that a problem?"

"No, but for safety reasons, I do prefer guests snorkel in pairs if they can." He looked back out toward the horizon. "The snorkeling around the boat is very good too. If you stay close, I could help if you run into trouble."

"I'm swimming with her," said William as he strode up behind the guide. He'd removed his shirt and now wore nothing but a pair of board shorts that rode low on his hips, showing off his toned abs to perfection. I clenched my thighs together as parts of me that needed to stay dormant stirred to life. "I needed to reapply my sunscreen first. She was going to wait for me nearby."

My eyes flickered up from that little trail of hair that disappeared under William's waistband. I was what?

The guide grinned. "No worries, mate. I just didn't want her to cut her leg on some coral or bump a sea urchin and not have help."

William nodded. "I appreciate it." He watched the guy make his way back toward the helm of the boat before he sat next to me. "Sorry if I overstepped. I didn't like how he stared at your ass when you walked over here."

"Is there a good way to look at my ass?" I laughed and crossed my arms over my chest.

He leaned a little closer. "Well, there's a quick glance when a man takes notice and there's the full-on leer that a man gets when considering whether or not he'd like to tap that later. Let's just say he didn't do the first."

"Ah, okay." Even though my cheeks were already warm from the sun, they heated up more. "Thank you, then. I'm not the tapping type."

His deep chuckle made my breath hitch in my chest. Why did I always have that reaction? Maybe it would eventually go away. "I didn't think you were." He nudged me with his elbow. "So, let's see some fish and whatever else is out there. I believe the brochure said we might find some eels and some small sharks too."

"Sounds good to me." We put on our masks and fins and slipped into the water. I pointed to where the reef rose closer to the surface, and William gave me a thumbs up before leading the way.

We explored every place the guide stopped, and I can't imagine we missed a thing. We saw all sorts of colorful coral and fish, sea stars, some eels, a sea turtle, and even a manta ray. The day was one of the most amazing experiences of my twenty-eight years and William proved to be the perfect person to share it with. He had a wicked sense of humor, was protective of me when it was warranted, and ensured I was never alone when Ghazi, our guide, came around. Ghazi, as the day wore on, became a bit odd. I was thankful William was there as a buffer.

On the ride back to the resort, we both laid our towels out on the boat deck and enjoyed the sun. By the time we arrived, we had exactly enough time to return to our villas, shower, and change before dinner would start serving in the restaurants.

After the boat was tied off, William helped me climb onto the dock, and we fell into step, heading in the direction of our rooms just like the night before. This silent hum filled the air between us. "Would you like to share a table for dinner again tonight?" he asked. When I turned, his eyebrows were lifted while the breeze played with his dark curls.

Definitely not an invitation to go on a date, but I enjoyed his company and talking with him over a glass of wine sounded like a much better way to end the day than eating on my own. "Sounds great. Where do you want to go?"

"I really enjoyed the grill last night. We could do that again or try something new. I overheard someone on the boat today rave about the more casual place by the pool."

I bit my lip while I considered the two options. "More than one of the entrees at the restaurant last night sounded incredible, and I really love the view."

"Good," he said, watching the pier while he walked. "You made the reservation last time, so I'll make one as soon as I get back."

"You better." I couldn't help the little flirting comments, but I'd probably never see him again once I returned home. I wouldn't think about it too much. I was here to enjoy myself, not overanalyze everything.

My villa was just ahead, so I skipped down the dock and grinned back at him before I hurried inside, shut the door, and rested against it. "Settle down, Ellie. You're probably in the 'friend zone,' so you don't need to get so worked up over him. He'll find some long-legged blonde in a couple of days and move on to greener pastures."

I pulled myself away and kicked off my flip flops by the wall. "But it doesn't mean I can't enjoy his company while I can."

I was putting on my strappy sandals when someone knocked. I fastened the ties around my ankle and rushed to open the door, finding William on the other side.

"I made the reservation for six. We have fifteen minutes. Are you ready?"

"Yes." I turned and peered about the room, shook my head, and walked back to the door. "I'm so used to carrying a purse, but since the meals get charged to the room, I don't need it, do I?"

"I don't see why you would. You just need the card key for your room."

I grabbed it from the nearby table and put it in my pocket. "Let's go."

We chatted about some of the creatures we'd seen snorkeling until we sat down at the same table as the night before. "I'm surprised we're sitting in the same place," I said offhand.

He gave a one-shouldered shrug. "I requested it. It has a great view of the ocean, so I didn't see any reason to sit somewhere else." He sat forward and rubbed his hands up and down his legs two or three times. "I had an idea while I was in the shower." I lifted my eyebrow, and he laughed and shook his head. "Not that kind of idea! I simply thought that since we're both here on our own, we could take the same tours and spend our vacations with each other. What do you think?"

"What if I want to have a completely lazy day and veg in my room watching chick flicks and ordering room service?"

His eyes narrowed a little before he grinned, making my stomach do that ridiculous flip flop it always did. "I suppose if you wanted to do that, I could spend a day on my own. Who knows? After a week, I might want to join you." We both laughed. "I want to go fishing, but I also want to go jet skiing. Which do you prefer for tomorrow?"

No thought or pause was required before I answered. "Jet skiing without question. I'm not much of a fisherman, though I will try it if you like."

"You've fished before?"

"Not deep sea or anything. My dad used to take me to a local lake, and we'd fish together. He had only girls, and I didn't gross out like my sister, Jena. I guess he thought I'd be better company. I never caught anything we could keep, though I did catch a boot once."

He laughed, sat back, and relaxed. "Then, I'll owe you. If you fish with me then you can pick some outing you wish, and I'll have to go with you."

The server approached our table, and we ordered a bottle of wine. When he left, I pressed my hands together in front of me. "I know exactly what you can do."

His only response was a wary sidelong look.

"So much has been on the internet and in the news about all of the plastic in the oceans. The concierge gave me a contact for an ocean clean-up group in the area. I intended to email the director tomorrow morning and set up a day or two to go volunteer." His tense shoulders relaxed almost immediately, and I smiled. "You thought I would pick something terribly girly, didn't you?"

"I didn't expect this, but it sounds interesting. Count me in."

"Good," I said as I dropped my hands to my lap and fiddled with my napkin. "I'm sure they'll appreciate one more able body to help."

I was pathetic! I went on vacation to relax, and now, I was destined to follow this guy around like a dog in heat. I was dying. By the end of the vacation, I'd be so sexually frustrated, who knew what I'd do! Did they have stores to buy a battery-operated boyfriend out here in the middle of the ocean? I'd never used one, but surely it was less embarrassing to purchase one of those than to slobber all over him? Wasn't it?

Chapter 3

The next morning, William knocked on my door at about nine. When I peeked out into the bright morning light, his sexy, crooked little grin and dimples greeted me. "I booked the jet skis for ten. Have you eaten breakfast? If you haven't, we could go down together before we set out."

"Not yet. Give me a minute so I can grab my bag."

I was dressed and ready to go, so I snagged my crochet bag by the handle and swung it around to my shoulder while I scooted into my flip flops. When the door closed behind me, I fell into step beside him.

"So, have you ever been on a jet ski?" he asked. He walked with the same gait as the last two days, head forward, looking at the view, with his hands in his pockets.

"No. Have you?"

"Yes, when I was sixteen. My family went on vacation to Mexico and my mom took me out for the day."

I smiled while I enjoyed the view of the muscles that his t-shirt didn't cover. Had he been as hot as this as a teenager? My eyes traced the broad shoulders he probably didn't possess until his twenties. "Tell the truth. How well do you remember how to do it?"

He turned and his eyes met mine with a slight turn up on one side of his lips. Had he caught me looking? "Vaguely. I'll definitely need a refresher course."

I couldn't help but laugh as we walked to the more casual restaurant where the resort served breakfast, boasting a buffet for those seated outdoors as well as inside. William took my bag from my shoulder. "Go ahead and grab a plate while I find us a table."

"Are you sure?"

He nodded. "I assume you'd rather sit outside."

"Of course." I grinned as he walked away, letting myself enjoy the view of his butt in board shorts for a moment first. As much as I didn't want to tear my eyes away, I also didn't want to get caught! Food, Ellie! Start thinking about food!

After I picked out my breakfast, I found him sitting at a table along the edge of the deck. "Great table," I said, setting down my plate.

"It was pure luck. An elderly couple saw me take your bag and assumed I was your husband." He chuckled and shrugged. "I admit to not correcting them when they offered me their place since they were finished."

I lifted an eyebrow. "That was rather dishonest of you."

He crossed his arms over his chest, one side of his lips quirking upward while his eyes darted to my lips and back. "Do you want to give up the table?"

"No way!" I dropped into the closest chair. "Go get your food. I promise not to give away your seat while you're gone."

He shook his head as he walked off. As I savored a bite of fresh mango, a waiter placed two lattes on the table.

"I didn't order these."

The young man didn't blink. "The gentleman did, ma'am." He set down a small container filled with sugars and sweeteners and walked away.

When William returned, I pointed to the two steaming cups. "You ordered lattes?"

"You mentioned you'd ordered a latte when you told me that story about your sister and your friend. If you don't want it—"

"No, it's perfect. I just forgot I mentioned it is all."

He took his seat and loaded his fork with eggs. "So, you never told me where you're from, or are we going to be secretive about ourselves? If it makes a difference, I swear I'm not a psychopath."

I bit my lip, trying not to laugh. "I'm from a small town just outside of Charleston, South Carolina." I accentuated my natural accent with more of a drawl and batted my eyelashes.

His eyes brightened as he grinned. "You're not too far from me. I'm from Savannah."

Talk about a coincidence! At least if he was a serial killer, I hadn't told him exactly where I lived.

"Are you close enough to Charleston to plan weddings there?"

"Yes, we've organized weddings all over the area," I said. "Jena even planned a ceremony and reception at a client's vacation home near Myrtle Beach."

"Is Jena a lot like you?"

I rolled my eyes. "Not at all. Jena is tall, while if you haven't noticed, I tend to shop in the petite department. She also has blonde hair with blue eyes. She's gorgeous. She doesn't ask for the attention yet men tend to gravitate toward her."

"You don't think you compare?"

"No," I said, shaking my head.

"Not every man wants a tall blonde, you know. You're beautiful—striking, in fact, in your own way."

I couldn't speak and practically gawked at him until he glanced down at his breakfast and said, "What about your friend?"

I shook myself out of it and laughed. "Charlie and I are nothing alike in looks or personality. She's the athlete of the group, she can swear like a sailor, and she's loyal to a fault."

"And she's a partner in a business that plans weddings?" he said, his voice a bit higher pitched.

"She started out just taking care of the books. She's gradually taken on more of the planning, and now, takes clients from time to time. She can control her cussing when she tries."

He held my gaze. "You care for both of them a lot. I can tell by the way you speak of them."

"Of course, I do. They're my best friends," I said. "Don't you have a best friend?"

"When I was younger and in college. I suppose, lately, my father has been more of my best friend."

"The two of you are close?"

He swallowed the bite he was chewing. "We weren't always, but we are now."

"That's nice." I honestly meant it and watched him to be certain he understood. The corners of his mouth curved upward and he nodded. It was good enough.

Somehow, we ended up on less personal topics until we were finished eating. Once I'd pushed back my plate, he rubbed his hands together. "Are you ready to hit the water?"

"Definitely." I grabbed my bag from where it hung on my chair and put it on my shoulder as I stood. "Lead the way."

The hut was a quick walk down the beach, and fortunately, the man who worked there proved to be great at giving a crash course in jet skis for dummies. They had a locker for our belongings, and without much fuss, we were out cruising along that aquamarine water in no time.

Jet skiing was a blast. If you counted how far we went in miles, I'd be willing to bet we zoomed around the entire island more than once. On numerous occasions, we teased one another by spraying each other. We made sure we didn't take any risks, but it was too much fun to soak William and snap him out of his serious side. It was an amazing day, though I still preferred snorkeling. However, spending my time with a handsome hunk was definitely no hardship!

I blinked a few times and sighed. Why was I out on a boat at six in the morning? I sipped my iced coffee and watched the horizon from behind my large, round sunglasses. The view of the water and sun-bleached sand in the distance hadn't gotten old . . . as if it could ever get old! Aside from dragging myself from bed before the sun rose, I was perfectly content. I settled in under the warmth of the early morning sunshine and sipped my drink.

"Are you ready to try fishing?"

I peered over my shoulder to William, who held an enormous fishing pole in one hand and a small fish in the other while he baited the hook. I scrunched my nose. "How about after I finish my coffee?" Maybe I should've gone snorkeling again.

He gave a deep chuckle that vibrated through my body. "You're such a girl."

"That's right," I said with some attitude. "And I like being that way. I enjoy pretty dresses, perfume, and makeup. Do you have a problem with it?" I took a sip of my drink while I propped my feet on the railing of the boat.

"Not at all." He stepped up to the edge as he finally hooked the bait on the line, then he cast it off the back of the boat, his muscular arms flexing and shifting as he moved the pole in a graceful arc. We sat in silence for a while. That was one thing I remembered from fishing with my dad—that you didn't talk while you fish. He always claimed it scared the fish away. Since this boat sat higher than the pier I fished on with my dad, I doubted the fish would be frightened away as easily, but I didn't want to ruin William's chances of catching something.

I tipped my head back, basking in the sun. The silence that surrounded us was only disturbed by the gentle breaking of the water on the hull of the boat and the cry of a gull occasionally passing overhead. I let my head loll to one side and found William facing me. He gave a tight smile before his line of sight shifted back to his fishing pole.

"Something wrong?" I asked a bit drowsily.

He cleared his throat while he concentrated on what he was doing. "No, not at all."

We fell into a comfortable silence and my eyes drifted closed. I must've dozed off for a while, because the next thing I knew, I startled at William's voice and the guide's loud commands. I sat up just in time to see William haul in a large tuna with an enormous grin on his face.

"Woah! Nice catch!" I said loudly so it carried over the noise on the deck.

"Thanks!" He waggled his eyebrows while he finished reeling in the line. "When are you going to catch a fish of your own?"

"I doubt there are any fishies who want to be caught by me." I lifted that one eyebrow before William became distracted by the guide removing the tuna from the hook.

When William cast out another line with fresh bait, I sat up and stretched my stiff muscles that were protesting from sitting too long in one position. I needed to do something besides sleep all day. I did tell William I'd give fishing a try! Before he could take his seat, I brushed my hands against one another. "Do you have a rod for me?"

He grinned while the guide fetched another pole and William handed me the bait. As much as I wanted to only handle the slimy little fish with two fingers, I didn't want the two men to laugh at me any more than they already had.

"Not like that. Let me help you."

After he propped his pole, his arms wrapped around me while he taught me to attach the small fish to the hook. I swallowed hard when my back brushed against the solid muscles of his chest, my skin pebbling at the brief contact. While they'd handled William's fish, I'd shed my cover-up in favor of my bikini top, so the feeling of his athletic body pressed to my back made it even harder not to quiver in my flip flops. He wrapped an arm around my waist and helped me cast. How was I supposed to hold the fishing rod when I couldn't stop trembling?

After he released me, he stripped off his shirt, making me clamp my jaw shut and pray that the excess of saliva that suddenly appeared in my mouth wasn't creating a river down my chin. This wasn't the first time I'd seen him shirtless. It also wasn't the first time I'd tried to pretend it had no effect on me.

"It's a beautiful day." He spoke softly as he sat down next to me.

"The extra clouds are nice today. It's still warm, but we get a few more breaks from the sun."

"What do you want to do for dinner tonight?"

I shrugged, eased back into my chair, and crossed my legs, clenching them together. His soft tone combined with the lack of shirt did things to my body. "We haven't made reservations. Why don't we try out the casual restaurant? Honestly, I'd love a burger."

He gave a quick dip of his chin with a smile. "A burger sounds awesome."

"Really?"

"Yes, really. I've enjoyed the fine dining, but I'd love something more every day."

I turned my attention back to my pole as we fell once again into a companionable silence. The problem was that I couldn't relax. Whether I was looking at him or not, I knew he was shirtless . . . beside me—a fact that made me squirm in my seat more than once.

When we returned to the resort, I took a thorough shower to get the stale fish smell off of me. We'd swam off the back of the boat for an hour before we returned, but I swear I could still smell the bait. I was probably paranoid, but a shower with some girly smelling shower gel was definitely in order!

Overall, the day was nice. I was able to watch the sea life, even though I failed miserably at catching any of it. William exhibited a tremendous amount of patience helping me bait my hook and with casting. I didn't even catch a boot but I blame my failure on distraction. Having that toned, tanned skin buffet right there at arm's length wreaked havoc with my concentration.

We were dining casually, yet I still put on my white sundress with the blue embroidery. I wasn't lying when I said I liked pretty and girly dresses and shoes. We might be going out for burgers, but I would be feminine doing it.

I'd just finished my makeup when a knock came from the door. I opened it to William dressed in his usual khaki shorts and a navy polo top that made his eye color pop even more than usual.

"You're dressed up," he said. His eyes dropped to my dress but didn't linger. They shot right back to my face. Yup, I was definitely in the friend zone.

"I told you I like dresses. I brought some shorts and some tops too, but I've always preferred dresses. If you don't like it, I can change." Why did I say that? It implied that I wanted to look nice for him. We weren't a couple! We were friends. Friends, Ellie! Friends!

He shook his head. "You look great, and I'm hungry. Let's go."

I grabbed my bag and followed him out to the walkway, my eyes watching the shift of his shorts while he walked. Damn! I was in big trouble!

Chapter 4

For the last two days, William had knocked at my door, but this morning, I knocked at his. I'd planned our activity for the day, so I had to get him out of his suite so we could be on our way. While I waited for him to answer, I glanced back at my villa. Was William the angry voice from my first day? Our huts were close enough to each other that it was entirely possible. The voice when he approached the maître d' that first night resembled the phone call I'd overheard. If the voice was his, he said he'd been making business calls—not that his work was any of my business.

When he came to the door, he wore nothing but a pair of khaki cargo shorts. I took a deep, heaving breath as that spattering of dark chest hair and those abs I enjoyed ogling disappeared under a forest green Polo. He grabbed the key to his room, his wallet from the table, and fastened his brown leather sandals onto his feet.

"Alright, I'm ready."

We made the boat in plenty of time and settled in for the ride to one of the local islands. The trip lasted about an hour, but we couldn't talk because of how fast we were moving. The few times we tried to speak or pointed to something out in the water we'd had to yell to be heard. More than a "Look!" wasn't worth the effort, otherwise, we'd have been hoarse by the time we reached our destination. Even so, that buzz that vibrated through me whenever he was close made me acutely aware of exactly where he was.

Upon our arrival, William handed me out of the boat and the guide from the resort pointed us in the direction of our destination, the local market. Most of the stalls had tropical fruit, vegetables, or even local fishermen selling their early morning catch, but a number of them had items more geared toward the tourists.

I stopped at one with swaths of brightly colored fabric hanging from poles and hooks everywhere. "How pretty!"

William stepped up behind me and fingered a few of them, his arm brushing my shoulder sending a jolt through me. "This would be a great gift for my sister. I can't come back from a trip without getting her something."

"How old is she?"

He pulled a geometric pattern from the cluster in front of him. "She's twenty. She attends Boston Conservatory."

"That's a bit of an age difference." I pulled a floral piece and handed my money to the man. "Do you have any other brothers or sisters?"

After he paid for his, he handed his to me to put in my crochet bag with mine. "We're eleven years apart. After I turned two, my parents tried to have another baby, but they weren't successful until years later when Addy came along."

"That must've been difficult on your parents."

"My mother more than my father," he said. He motioned around us. "Where to next?"

I pointed down a different path. "This way." We started walking again, taking in the colorful buildings and homemade wares around us. "Is Addy short for Addison?"

His lips curved to one side. "Adelaide, actually. She's named for my maternal great-grandmother."

"Pretty. I like old and different names. It seems like naming a baby these days has become so trendy."

His dimples appeared as he smiled and nodded. "I've always liked my mother's name—Freya."

I stopped and turned to him. "I've never heard that one. Do you know its origin?"

"Freya was the Norse Goddess of love, beauty, and fertility. My mother was British and it's a fairly popular name in England." He cleared his throat. "She died six years ago. Cervical cancer."

I put my hand to my chest. "Oh, I'm so sorry."

William shook his head while he studied his feet. "I miss her every day, and I've avoided speaking of her for so long. I had kind of a self-destructive phase after her death. I'm really just coming out of it, I think. Don't feel bad that asked me about her. You couldn't have known, and honestly, I find I don't mind speaking of her with you."

"Maybe because you barely know me," I said as he caught my eyes.

"No, we've talked a lot the last few days. I think I know more about you than some people I've known for years." His gaze held mine for a moment or two before the coward in me turned my head and started walking through the market again. Torturing myself was one thing, but God only knew what William was thinking. A vacation hook-up was a bad idea . . . or was it? Was I that desperate and horny? It'd been almost two years since I'd last had sex, and I'd barely dated. Most men didn't make it past the first evening out. They either wanted more than I was willing to give so early in a relationship or they were a loser—no job, no ambition, and no interest in behaving like an adult instead of an overgrown high schooler.

We moved into a more crowded section of the market, so William shifted ahead. A second later, a hand wrapped itself around mine, making me look down to William's fingers entwined with my own. Once he'd steered us through, I expected him to let go, but he didn't, and I had to concentrate to keep from staring at that point where our bodies met. The most disconcerting part was this slight tingle that traveled from him and almost radiated through me. It might have been my imagination, but I swear I could feel it in my toes. I kept waiting for him to drop my hand like it stung him, but instead, his palm remained pressed flush to mine until we stopped at one of the street vendors and bought some lunch. Once we had our food, we sat on a bench close by to eat.

"Tomorrow we're on trash patrol, right?" he said after swallowing his first bite.

I rolled my eyes while I finished unwrapping my food. "Yes, it's the easiest day for them to pick us up on the way. We're going to clean up an island west of here. If we have time, we might put on some snorkeling gear and check the reef nearby."

"Are we just volunteering the one day?" he asked with his brow furrowed. "I know I joke about it, but I do admire that you want to take time out of your vacation for something worthwhile."

The compliment caught me off-guard. When he'd spoken, the teasing drawl to his voice made me miss the sincerity of his words. I should've known he wasn't seriously putting the project down. "Thanks." His flattery still made my cheeks heat up. I couldn't look at him at that moment so I stared down at my food like it was an impossibly riveting chapter of a book.

"Um, they're cleaning up another island in this area next week. I told them we're interested but we aren't certain of our schedule yet. I thought I'd email them closer in and finalize things."

"Okay." He waved a hand in front of my eyes. "Ellie, are you alright? You're so quiet all of a sudden."

I dropped my head back against the wall behind me but turned so I could see his face. His forehead wrinkled and his eyebrows drew down in the middle while he watched me. "I'm fine."

"Are you sure?"

"Positive." I straightened and scanned the square, ready to change the subject. I didn't want to discuss why a compliment from him made me blush. "I still need to find a gift for Jena and Charlie."

He pointed down the other alley. "We can check out the other row of stalls on our way back to the boat."

I peered down the narrow aisle. "Hopefully, they have something. Jena isn't so difficult, but Charlie is always a pain in the ass to buy gifts for."

We wiped our hands on our napkins and tossed the trash before heading in the direction William pointed. I found a bracelet for Jena and windchimes made of seashells for Charlie before we returned to the docks. Once we were on the boat, we had to wait a while for the rest of our group to return before we could head back.

When we stood outside my villa, William scratched the back of his neck. "Look, I'm not really in the mood to eat out tonight."

"Oh, okay." My stomach sank. I really didn't want to eat by myself. I'd gotten used to him joining me. I enjoyed his company.

"Would you want to order room service?" he asked. "We can eat at one of our villas?" As it had turned out, his room was only two down from mine, which had made getting together for our day trips much easier. "Would that be okay?"

I nodded as the tension in my shoulders ebbed away. "Yeah, it sounds nice. If you'd stayed in, I would've probably ordered room service anyway."

"You're sure?"

I nodded and backed toward the door. "I am. The market was pretty busy. I'd welcome some peace and quiet."

"I'm going to drop off my gift for Addy, and I'll come back so we can go over the menu."

"See you in a bit then." My body hummed when I turned and went inside, but why? Had he watched me or was it nervous energy about him coming to my villa? It was just dinner. I took a deep breath in an attempt to quash the butterflies circling around my stomach. We were friends and nothing more. I needed to keep repeating that to myself. I couldn't let myself forget.

The presents I'd purchased were quickly stowed in my suitcase before I checked my appearance in the mirror. I'd given up having my hair down in curls except for dinner. All of the boat rides made it impossible unless I wanted a knotted rat's nest on my head. Today's fishtail looked a little windblown but not too bad. If we were staying in, I also wouldn't need to change out of the denim cutoffs and lacy white top that covered my white and blue patterned bikini.

For comfort, I took off my simple opal necklace, the matching bracelet, and ring I always wore, as well as my watch and lastly, my earrings, and put them in a small bowl on the bathroom counter. I was unfastening my sandals when a knock echoed through the room. I set my shoes by the wall and let William in.

He shut the door behind him and held up a pair of fins, a mask, and a snorkel. "It's still pretty early. I thought we could explore off the deck while we wait for the food."

"Cool idea," I said, taking his gear and putting it outside where mine, on loan from the resort, rested against the wall.

When I'd returned, he'd pulled out the menus and laid them on the bed. "I suppose we could order from different places if we wanted."

I put the menu for Salt Water to the side. "The food is great, but I want something different."

"Why don't we finally have Asian. You know, when in Asia."

I laughed and covered my mouth for a moment before I said, "Oh! That was bad."

"I know. It made you laugh, though." His dimples peeked through and a curl fell over his forehead. "How about Thai? We haven't tried that yet?"

He called in our order once we'd decided. If they found it odd that he charged it to his room, but had it delivered to another, they didn't seem to comment.

While he was on the phone, I took off my shorts and top and threw them over a chair so I was ready to swim when he was done. He'd been reading the menu while he ordered, but when his eyes darted up, they didn't shift back to the menu as he told them his choice. One second, he looked at my face, and the next, his gaze was trained on my feet. Had that been a covert attempt at checking me out? He'd never seemed very affected by me so I shrugged it off. I was making things into more than they were. I had to be.

When he hung up, he shrugged off his polo and smiled. "Are you ready?"

The water was just as clear and blue off the small porch of my villa as it was further out, and it was so shallow, I could even touch the sand bottom with my feet. After swimming around for a while and picking up a few empty shells, I took off my snorkeling gear and let myself relax on my back and float.

"Was that a knock?"

Before I could stand, William hoisted himself up onto the deck, grabbed a towel, and disappeared inside. I took my time swimming back, so by the time he wheeled the room service cart to the porch, I'd barely climbed out of the water.

He handed me my towel, and I dried off while he moved the food to a small table in one corner. My stomach growled when I sat down, making him chuckle. "I'm glad the food came when it did. If you're that hungry, you might've eaten a fish straight from the water."

"Ha, ha," I said, even though I must've smiled at him like an idiot.

"How old are you?" He took his first bite of noodles while he watched me.

"Twenty-eight. You're thirty-one if I've done my math correctly from your sister's age?"

"And you saved for six years for this trip? Most people save for a house or a new car."

I shrugged a shoulder casually. "I'm happy renting my little apartment downtown, and I own a car that I don't have monthly payments on. I see no reason to change that at the moment. I do have a separate savings tucked away in case of emergencies."

"Not many people have a car without a loan or lease."

"Well, that's sort of complicated. A few years ago, when my parents divorced, they had a huge feud over the division of property. My mother wanted the house and her car, but she couldn't afford to pay my dad for his share of either. In the end, she gave up her car and my dad gave it to me."

His eyebrows did this cute thing where they dipped down in the middle. "From what you've told me, Jena is older, so why you?"

I swallowed the bite I was chewing. "That's why it's complicated. My mother always preferred Jena. She never tried to hide it and would tell anyone how Jena was more beautiful and more talented, etcetera, etcetera. She was furious when my dad gave me her car."

"What kind of car would he just give you like that?"

I scraped my teeth along my bottom lip. "A two-year-old Lexus RX450h."

William whistled his eyes big. "That's a nice car."

"It is. A part of me felt guilty about taking it from him. I offered to pay my dad what the car was worth, but he absolutely refused. He told me he'd sell it to a junkyard if I didn't use it. You see, my mother refused to help pay for me to go to college, so I busted my butt for scholarships and paid for the rest by working. My dad insisted the car was to make up for his lack of a spine. He always felt bad he didn't insist they help me get my degree."

"Where did you go to school?"

"I have a Bachelor's in Graphic Communications from Clemson."

"And you paid for it yourself." His fork sat forgotten in his food while he gaped at me.

"My first year, I had enough in scholarships and grants to cover everything. After that, I managed to get enough for most of the tuition. I worked on campus to earn the rest." I twirled my noodles around my fork. "I had a cushy job in the audio/visual department of the library. Mostly I studied while I monitored the desk."

"You don't sound bitter at all about it."

I lifted a shoulder. "It does me no good to hate my mother or blame my father. Charlie and I found a cheap apartment during the summer between our freshman and sophomore years which made it less expensive than living on campus. That was when we started putting money away to start our company. Jena also worked during school and saved everything she earned, and Charlie and I did the same. I managed to pick up some freelance graphic design jobs on top of working on campus, which helped out a lot. Jena had earned her diploma two years before me and worked for another wedding planner in Charleston until we graduated. We all moved back to Marysville and shared a studio apartment for the first three years after college until we had a solid foundation and clientele coming in." He continued to stare at me like I'd sprouted a second head, which made my insides twist like crazy. "Is something wrong?"

He startled and shook his head. "No, I'm sorry. I'm impressed." I must've been looking at him like I didn't believe him because he then started nodding. "Really, I am. Not many people are willing to put in the work you have to get what they want."

"Thank you." I finally put the bite I'd been twirling for the last five minutes in my mouth.

"So," he said with a grin. "Who's been your most challenging client?" I bit my lip and explained the worst bridezilla I'd had the misfortune to work for, the pain of overbearing future mothers-in-law, and a few catering mishaps. He laughed at the ridiculousness of a lot of the problems we faced, but he didn't poke fun. Instead, for the rest of dinner, he peppered me with questions about weddings and event planning.

Afterward, we rolled the room service cart outside the front door and returned to the water. It was getting dark and the sky had that incredible wash of purples, reds, and blues like it did every night. I still loved it. I floated onto my back again so I could enjoy it while William did the same beside me. We did use our hands to keep ourselves near the villa, but other than that, I settled in and enjoyed the absolute serenity of the moment.

When the sky became an amazing tableau of stars, William shifted and stood next to me. "Come on, let's sit on the deck for a while and finish the wine. I'm getting all pruney."

I laughed and followed. He held out his hand to help me up, and I'd barely planted my foot on the deck when it slipped out from under me. The next thing I knew, I was lying on top of William and guffawing at my own clumsiness. He shook with laughter too as he sat us both up.

Our eyes locked and the laughter faded into something else—something heavy that pulled at a spot deep in my chest. His darkened eyes darted down to my lips and my heart began to pound in a heavy rhythm against my sternum, making me feel odd and slightly dizzy.

Who closed the distance between us is anyone's best guess. One minute we couldn't stop staring at one another and the next our lips pressed and tangled together while every last bit of space between our bodies evaporated. My fingers curled into the hair at the nape of his neck while my other hand clenched the firm muscle of his shoulder, holding on for dear life while his kiss lit every cell of my body on fire.

He groaned and grasped my ass, pulling me closer until his hard length pressed against my core. God, how I ached for him! I ground down against him and all that heat under his board shorts, gasping into his mouth at the tension that began to coil in my belly. It wouldn't take much—not much at all for him to tip me over that edge. I'd never been so turned on in my life. His hands seared my flesh like branding irons as his tongue darted in and grazed mine.

His palm slid up my back and tangled in my bikini ties just before he suddenly wrenched himself away. "Oh, God!" His eyes squeezed shut as his hands fell to my thighs. "I'm sorry. I can't do this . . . we can't do this."

I pulled myself from his lap, plopping ungracefully on the deck right before he stood, grabbed his shirt, and rather than swimming to his own villa from the deck, he barreled out of the door.

Chapter 5

Should I knock? I bit my bottom lip as I stood in front of William's door. I hadn't spoken to him since he abruptly left my villa the night before. I'd ordered breakfast to my room, but I hadn't been able to eat a bite because my stomach was tied in dozens of jumbled knots. How I hoped things weren't awkward after what happened between us! I rapped three times on his door, and after a minute or two, he finally opened it and gave me a quick glance before he closed and locked it up behind him.

Dark circles under his eyes made their vibrant blue stand out even more than normal. He must've tossed and turned all night like I had. I'd moved around so much, I became impossibly tangled in the sheets. Cold showers were *not* the perfect thing right before bed. Hopefully, I would never have to do that again! Not that the icy water helped in the slightest. My body never really turned off after last night, so I still ached in places I didn't usually talk about in public.

The boat with the conservation group logo pulled up to the dock five minutes after we arrived, and we hopped on board before it took off toward the horizon. William sat next to me, just like always, but his behavior was strikingly different than the last few days. He'd hardly looked at me since I knocked on his door, and he hadn't spoken a single word. The tension between us crackled. Just what I needed! I came to paradise to relax and ended up in the middle of a drama I couldn't understand. We needed to talk, but this wasn't the time or the place. I would push when we had some privacy. If he didn't avoid me. The simple fact was I couldn't allow him to avoid me. We had to clear the air.

An hour later, we pulled as close to the shore of a small island as we could, dropped anchor, and piled out. The leader of the group, Rob, came over, gave us bags, and told us how everything worked with the different bags for trash and recyclables. William walked ahead of me, silent of course, while he gathered plastic bottles and other trash. I sighed and followed a few paces behind and closer to the water.

"How's it going?" asked Rob after he'd checked on the rest of the volunteers.

I slowed and turned to face him. "Really well, I think."

He smiled and started picking up some bottles right at the water line. "I really admire that you and your friend wanted to spend part of your vacation helping clean up."

"Thank you. I've seen the pictures and videos of the pollution online and have been eager to pitch in and do something, so I'm glad tracked down your group. If you let me know when you'll be cleaning up another beach in this area, William and I would like to volunteer again. Maybe next week?"

"We'd love to have you. We never turn down free help," he said animatedly. "I'll email you on Monday, so we can arrange another day."

"Thanks. I appreciate it."

"So, where are you from? There's an accent there, but I can't place it."

"Marysville, South Carolina. It's right outside of Charleston."

He picked up some netting and put it in his bag. "Not too far from the water then?"

I smiled and shrugged. "Not too far, I suppose. I actually don't go to the beach much when I'm home. We used to go to Myrtle Beach when I was young, but a lot of that coast is pretty touristy during the summer."

"Do you have a local conservation group that cleans the beaches there?"

"We probably do, but I honestly never thought to check into it. Thanks for the idea."

Rob paused and tilted his head a fraction. "It's understandable. Most people see the videos and photographs of the beaches in Indonesia, Malaysia, and other tropical locations. They don't think of the impact closer to home. Every bit makes a difference."

Something niggled at me, making me look over my shoulder. My eyes met William's, but he immediately looked down and started working his way further up the waterfront.

"How long have the two of you been together?"

My head whipped around at Rob's question. "Oh, we're just friends. We actually met earlier this week, not long after we both arrived. We're both on our own and interested in most of the same activities, so we decided to team up for our vacations." I let my eyes peek back at William. If he was listening, I couldn't tell.

"Interesting," said Rob. "I meet a number of tourists—you can't help it living and working here—but that's the first time I've heard of strangers spending their holiday together."

"He's been a little quiet today, but he's a good guy."

Someone called out, so Rob hurried off to take care of whatever issue they were having while I continued on my current path, cleaning the edge where the water lapped up and receded, trying to catch bits of trash before they washed back out into the ocean. The island was tiny, so by the time we met with the group who walked in the opposite direction, it was lunchtime. The boat traveled around to meet us, and once everything was loaded up, we started our return.

William sat beside me, once again without saying a freaking word. The man wouldn't even point out a bird or something interesting in the water. It was odd to be with him but not really be with him, if that made sense.

When we pulled up to the resort, I rose from my seat and Rob opened the gate so I could step out to the dock. "Thanks for helping," he said, holding out his hand. "I'll email you about another day."

I nodded while I shook his hand. "Thank you. I'd appreciate it. I enjoyed taking part. I look forward to your email." I stepped away from the boat, but Rob called my name, making me turn back.

He walked up to me until he was really kind of close. "Would you like to have dinner sometime?"

I'm sure I looked like a fish with my mouth gaping open. I hadn't expected him to ask me out at all. Had he given off any clues? If he had, I'd never noticed.

Before I could respond, I stumbled to the side from someone—well, William—pulling my hand. "Sorry, she has plans," he said gruffly.

"I'm sorry!" I called as William tugged me in the direction of the villas like a caveman.

Rob waved and shook his head. Since he seemed like a pretty laid-back guy, I doubt he was mad, but I was definitely about to explode, and the sight wasn't going to be pretty. I wrenched my hand from William. "You didn't have to be so rude."

He stopped so quickly, I almost ran into him. "Why? Did you want to go out with him?"

"Whether I did or not is irrelevant! We aren't seeing one another. I don't have a boyfriend, so why should it matter if I go to dinner with him or not?" I pivoted on my heel and strode toward my villa. William could kiss my ass if he thought he could tell me what to do!

I didn't have to look behind me to know he followed. His heavy footfalls on the dock let everyone with a villa nearby know he was passing.

I swung my door shut behind me, but it didn't slam as expected. Shit! He'd followed me inside? I shook I was so angry. "What do you think you're doing?" I said as I turned, crossing my arms over my chest.

"Did you want to go out with him?"

"What difference does it make?"

"It makes a difference to me!" He raked his fingers through his dark windswept curls.

"You didn't even say hello this morning." My voice had dropped to a dangerously low pitch, but he didn't know that. He'd never been subjected to my temper in the past. It was a good thing Jena wasn't here to warn him. "You didn't speak to me the entire morning, and now, you want to dictate whether or not I go to dinner with someone. I don't think so!"

"Ellie," he said with a drawl.

"No, I don't know what was so objectionable about what happened last night, but you could talk to me instead of playing the quiet game like a little boy."

"I'm not a child." His jaw clenched along with the fists he held at his sides.

"Really? You behaved like a petulant one today."

"Because this is fucking difficult! Because I want you, but I can't do anything about it! I . . ."

"You what?"

"My life is complicated right now."

I covered my face for a moment and dropped my hands, so they slapped against my legs. "Whose isn't? Would you please leave? I think I'll eat dinner on my own tonight."

"Ellie." His voice held this quality that made the hair on my arms stand on end.

I slowly backed from him, but before I could go far, he swooped forward, wrapped an arm around my waist, burrowed his fingers into my hair, and claimed my lips—hard. My knees buckled, but I grabbed his shoulders and held on tight as he deepened the kiss, his tongue dipping into my mouth to tease mine.

My hands drifted to his waist where I tugged at his t-shirt until it came free of his cargo shorts. When I slipped my hands beneath the soft cotton, he released my lips and gasped, grasping his shirt and pulling it over his head. He tossed it to the side as my fingertips drifted along the ripples of his abs and around to his back. He wasn't big or crazy sculpted, but he worked out and it showed.

He picked me up by my butt cheeks, and I wrapped my legs around his waist. I needed to get closer—so close that we were nearly fused together. My heart beat so fast I was lightheaded, and I panted more like I'd sprinted a mile than simply being carried to the bed.

When my back met the mattress, his warm breath prickled my skin while he trailed his nose along my cheek to plant one or two suckling kisses starting right below my ear. My body curled into his as he made his way to my collarbone, grazing the ridge with his teeth. How could he do this? How could he render me incapable of doing nothing more than drowning in the ache and burn he incited with his mouth and his hands?

My top soon joined his on the floor, then he drew himself up on his knees so he straddled my hips and pulled the bikini string at the back of my neck. I lifted and reached behind me to untie the one between my shoulder blades. When my top dropped away, he groaned and feathered his fingers along the underside of one of my breasts.

"God, you're perfect." His voice came out all raspy and sexy as hell. Before I could second guess my decision, I grabbed the back of his neck and pulled him down for another scorching kiss. My hips refused to remain still and my legs squeezed his hips tightly while he pressed me down into the mattress, his chest coming flush with mine as he sucked in a breath.

Our eyes didn't waver as I cupped his cheek with my palm. A part of me ached so badly, all I wanted was to skip all of this and have him buried deep inside me. At the same time, I couldn't. This was William. He felt familiar, like I'd known him forever. Something in me needed to savor every moment.

He trailed small kisses down my neck, pressing his lips between my breasts and to the underside of one before he took the nipple in his mouth. When he suckled hard, my eyelids fluttered closed again as my fingers clenched his hair.

He trailed his tongue from one nipple to the other while his hand suddenly slipped under the thin barrier of my bikini bottoms and touched me, making my back arch off the bed. "Oh, please," I whimpered.

The cool air hit me when my shorts and bikini bottoms joined the rest of my clothes. William licked his fingers with a wicked grin, his hand returning to my core, causing me to make noises that would make a porn star proud—not that I cared in the slightest! He hit this spot just inside while he caressed the outside until the ache and the need and the burn that had been coiling inside me exploded. I cried out. I couldn't help it. I would've burst if I'd tried to hold it in.

While the orgasm helped, I wasn't nearly satisfied, and I wouldn't be until he was inside me—deep inside, relieving that unbearable throbbing. I reached for him, unbuttoning his shorts and pushing them and his boxer briefs over his hips. My fingers trailed a line down his pecs and his abs as he leaned forward to recapture my lips, but my hand didn't stop its exploration until it wrapped around his girth.

"Ellie," he said as he broke away. "I fucked up. I don't have a condom."

I let go of him long enough to scoot backwards and dig a box of condoms out of my suitcase. The last person I wanted to think about right now was Jena, but thank God she'd insisted I pack them!

I pulled a packet out before I haphazardly threw the rest on the bed and ripped open the foil wrapping, slipping it on him before he could take it from me. My legs wrapped around him when he covered his body with mine, and he hissed as he, one measured thrust at a time, filled me.

I always thought it a myth that you could feel like one with someone—as though you were connected so completely you couldn't tell where one ended and the other began. William proved it was real. I'd never burned for anyone the way I did for him. I never ached and needed them as I needed him. I wasn't the most experienced woman, but William put my past lovers to shame. They didn't even come close.

As he moved in and out of me, that low hum that vibrated through my body began to intensify and that burn where we met began to spread and tighten. I reached for him and kissed him while he continued to thrust, creating more friction than I could handle. My heels dug into the back of his thighs while my toes curled and my back arched like a bow. Did he even feel a fraction of the intensity I did? I could only hope it meant the same to him that it did to me. That was the last muddled thought before everything in me and around me shattered into a million pieces.

With one long last groan, he collapsed on top of me. His face burrowed against my shoulder as his lips grazed my neck. His weight pressing me down into the bed settled me and connected to me to him as much as the intimacy we'd just shared. I wrapped my arms around him, wanting to bask in the sensation for just a little bit longer.

When he stirred, I pressed my lips to his temple, and he inhaled deeply when his lips found mine. "Are you okay?"

I nodded and kissed him again. "Yes, I just feel very lazy right now."

He gave that low chuckle that made my insides all wobbly. "I know what you mean, but I should get up and throw away the condom."

"Leave it to the condom to spoil things."

He laughed and gave me one last kiss before he walked bare-assed naked into the bathroom. No matter how boneless I felt, I still lifted my head to watch him as he walked away. The view was definitely worth it.

"Are you hungry?" He asked when he re-entered the room.

"Starving! Should we order room service? I don't feel much like going out."

He took the portfolio from the desk while I sat up and pulled the sheet to cover my breasts. "No, me either."

I grabbed the menu for the Thai restaurant and lifted an eyebrow at him, making those dimples appear when he grinned. He called in the order and dropped the portfolio to the floor. When he leaned in closer, he brushed some loose curls behind my ear.

I caught his hand and kissed it. "When you said you couldn't because your life is complicated, what did you mean?" His smile faltered, and even though we should have discussed it before, at that moment, I wished I hadn't asked.

He sighed and trailed his finger along the top of the sheet, dipping between my breasts. "Can we pretend everything at home doesn't exist for now?"

"We have to go back eventually, you know."

His lips caressed the line of my shoulder to my ear. "I know, but you may decide I'm a moody ass, and you don't want anything to do with me by the end of next week."

A laugh bubbled from my throat. "I doubt that."

William drew back as his eyes met mine. "If we decide we want to continue this, we'll lay it all out and see how we proceed."

"We don't even live in the same state. How would that work?"

His large palm cradled my cheek. "I'd be willing to make it work. Would you?"

My eyes searched his. They didn't waver, they didn't seem to conceal anything, and they held mine so surely. I suppose I'd just have to trust him. "Yes, yes I would."

Chapter 6

I stretched my feet toward the foot of the bed and opened my eyes to my villa's amazing view of the water. William was spooned behind me, his arm wrapped around my stomach, keeping my entire backside pressed against him. We'd been busy yesterday . . . and last night . . . and early this morning.

It had been mid-afternoon before our lunch arrived yesterday, so we ate and talked before we tested out the mattress again, though not with the same urgency as the first time. William built me up slower and we took our time, savoring one another in a way we couldn't before.

After, we ordered a bottle of wine and a couple of appetizers then swam until they arrived. After we ate, we showered, though we didn't bathe each other until we played first.

I'd never in my life slept as well as I had last night—well, except when William woke me up sometime in the early morning. Normally, I like my sleep, but it didn't take much for him to convince me I'd rather let him coax my body fully awake, and it didn't take long for me to beg for him to finish what he'd started. Without much difficulty, I fell back to sleep, sated and snuggled against him.

"What time is it?" he mumbled into my ear.

"Eight-forty-five. Did you make any reservations for today?"

"Just one, but we don't have to be at the dock until eleven." He pressed his hips flush against my rear so I could feel that it was indeed morning—and promised to be a very good one. "What could we possibly find to do for the next two hours?"

"Gee, I wonder?" I laughed as his hand curled up and cupped my breast, teasing the nipple until it was painfully hard. "Maybe breakfast?"

"Maybe after." He pulled me onto my back and shifted on top while he kissed me. He brushed his lips down to my chin, nipping my neck, and grinned wickedly up at me just before he disappeared under the sheet. As his tongue took a lazy drag between my folds, I shuddered and lost interest in food. I didn't care if we ever ate again.

My hands slid down the sheets and found the top of his head, gripping his hair while he suckled that sensitive bit of flesh between his teeth and my back arched off the bed. "Oh, God!"

When his finger joined in and pressed up firmly, my eyes rolled back in my head, my brain lost all concept of what was going on around me, and that burn that started at his talented tongue began to spread until it engulfed me. I let out a sob. "William, please! I need you inside me now. I want you inside me when I come."

The next thing I knew, he was kissing me and filling me until I couldn't understand how I hadn't exploded already. He reached places no man ever had and not merely physically. His hands gripped my rear and pulled me into every stroke, not that I needed his help. I greedily wanted every inch he had to give me and more.

His face buried into my neck where he nipped at the tender flesh while he groaned in my ear. "Fuck, Elle. It's too much. I can't hold on much longer."

I'd been teetering close to that edge for a while, holding back until he joined me, but his words sent me diving into the abyss as he went rigid. I cried out and grasped his hips to make that delicious wave last for as long as possible for both of us.

"I can't move," he said against my shoulder.

"I think we need to bathe again."

His shoulders shook as he struggled to push himself up to hover over me. With an evil grin, he licked from my bellybutton to my neck. "Darn, now we definitely should clean up."

We showered again before he dressed and rushed back to his villa to change. I brewed coffee in my room, and once he returned with fresh board shorts and a t-shirt, we sat on the deck until we had to leave for whatever he'd planned.

After he closed the door, I backed away from him with a grin. "Are you going to tell me what we're doing?"

He lunged forward, lacing his fingers with mine. He had a slight lift to one side of his lips. "No, it's a surprise."

I grazed my teeth along my bottom lip trying not to smile like a fool. How long did it take someone to fall in love? People talked about love at first sight, whirlwind romances, and sometimes couples married after dating no more than a week or two. What made some relationships last fifty years and others last five days?

As much as I didn't want to fall too fast, that possibility seemed inevitable. William could be an ass when he wanted, but the moments that made me want to throw him down and kiss him occurred far more often than those mannerisms that made me want to slap him silly.

William walked to the concierge desk when we arrived at the main lodge. After speaking to the man on duty for a few minutes, he brought me to a dock on the other side of the building where a boat sat at the end of the pier.

"Are we the only ones booked for the tour?"

With an adorable crooked smile and a shrug, he handed me on board and followed behind. We sat on a cushioned bench to one side as the boat shifted away from the dock and out to sea. His fingers caught my stray curls as they whipped around my face and held them back while the knuckles of his other hand caressed a spot at the junction of my neck and shoulder. Goosebumps spread from that point down my back, making me shiver uncontrollably.

"Behave," I yelled back at him as we began speeding away from the resort. I may have said it, but a part of me would've been disappointed if he'd listened. Fortunately, he continued to touch me in some fashion. Nothing that would raise eyebrows, but enough to keep my body charged and ready to go.

We slowed after about ten minutes. William unlaced his fingers from mine and pointed. "Look."

I followed the direction of his finger to where a white patch of sand breaking the clear topaz of the water came into view.

"It's a sandbank." His lips tickled my ear as he whispered. "I thought we might have a picnic."

I peered over my shoulder at him. "Seriously?"

"Yeah, don't you like it?"

"No, I don't like it. I love it." I grabbed his cheeks and kissed him hard. "It's wonderful!"

"Good, let's go then." We took off our sandals, and he led me by the hand to the swimming platform, which they pulled as close to the sandbank as they could. Someone on the boat carried a huge cooler out for us while we waded to our own private island—for a few hours anyway.

We spread out a blanket, and William began rummaging through the food. "I thought we'd eat now. I'm hungry." He wore that same wicked grin from earlier, and my cheeks burned at the memory of me begging while he had that same curve to his lips, his hands and fingers working me up to a fevered pitch. It wasn't fair how little it took for him to make me so weak-kneed. He laid out fruit, some seafood dishes, and a loaf of bread. "Would you like some Prosecco?"

"Definitely." I ignored my body's reaction to that grin and relaxed back, basking in the warmth of the sun until I heard William's voice near my ear.

"Elle?"

"Hmm?" I opened my eyes to a full glass of wine in front of me. My fingers brushed his and he darted in for a quick kiss before he held a shrimp in front of my face.

"Open up."

I laughed while I sat up. "Are you serious? You want to feed me?" At his nod, I leaned forward and took the morsel, sucking the seasoning from his fingers. His eyes lit when I picked up another from the bowl and fed it to him. Even though it was tempting, we didn't feed each other the entire time. Okay, maybe most of the time.

We snorkeled a bit once we ate, we laid out on the blanket under the sun, and we flirted and played in the water. We had enough food, water, and wine to stay all afternoon. We didn't care in the slightest whether we were suitable for company. We had no one else around to offend. In fact, it was a good thing I wore sunblock since William splayed his hand on my stomach while we sunbathed. The last thing I needed to bring home was a large, obviously male handprint on my belly. If Jena and Charlie were to see it, I'd never hear the end of it.

"Is Ellie your given name or a nickname?"

I lazily opened my eyes. "My dad named me for my grandmother, Elenora. I suppose people thought my name was formal for a little scrap of a girl like me, so it got shortened and stuck." Everyone had always called me Ellie—that is until last night when William started calling me Elle. I loved that he'd given me a name only he used. It made my stomach do that twisty thing it always did when he gave that low throaty chuckle or grinned at me.

"Tell me something about yourself, something I don't know already." His voice was gravelly as though he'd just woken up.

I rolled to my side to face him. "I like to draw. I can draw some things really well but others—well, not so well. Most of my electives in college were extra art classes." His fingers made a lazy trail up and down my arm while his eyes held mine with such steadiness I had a difficult time not looking away. "Tell me something I don't know about you."

"I became licensed for green construction before I left on vacation. I've wanted to do it for a long time, but my father never saw the purpose. Since I'm now running the company on my own, I want to shift from the neighborhoods and planned communities we used to build to more custom designs. I also wouldn't mind conversions of older buildings."

"That's great!"

He dropped his head from his hand down to the blanket. "My dad isn't sold on it yet, but he's accepted that it's the direction I want to go."

I shifted up on my elbow so I looked down on him. "For what it's worth, I think it's amazing." Before I could react, he kissed me and took my hand, pulling me to stand. The next thing I knew, he hoisted me onto his shoulder.

"What are you doing?" I yelled, laughing. He waded out into the water then slid me down until we were both immersed to our shoulders in all that clear warm water.

"I think you're amazing." At his confession, my stomach erupted as though a million butterflies were flying in circles. "I've never felt this way before." He never blinked as the words came out at a whisper. His gaze stayed so open, like I could see every emotion as long as my eyes never left his.

"Me either."

His fingers trailed down my cheek as his lips brushed lightly against mine, the smell of the ocean and him mingling as I inhaled. Eager to taste him again, I pressed forward and darted my tongue against his lips. He groaned and let me inside. This was so perfect. He was perfect.

We spent the entire afternoon in our own secluded paradise. I'm sure we scared the fish away with what we did in the water, but they couldn't tell anyone what we'd done or where our hands wandered. I couldn't say without my cheeks flaming up in the process.

The boat came back to check in at pre-set intervals, but we didn't choose to return until almost dinnertime.

"Thank you for today," I said as we walked back to our villas.

"Wait until tomorrow."

"You think what you have planned is better than today?" I lifted my eyebrow in a silent challenge.

"Maybe not better, but I hope you'll like it."

I let the matter drop until we reached my villa. Once inside, away from prying eyes, I pushed him onto the bed, climbed up over his hips, and straddled him. I know he loved it. At over six foot, he could push my little five-foot-two self off if he really wanted.

"What do you have planned?" I lifted my eyebrow and waited.

"It's a surprise." He said it so smugly that I dug my fingers into his ribs. "Ow!" He squirmed and began to laugh. "I know how to tickle you, too, you know."

"Why can't you tell me?"

"Because . . . I wanted . . . to surprise you . . . like today. The look . . . on your face . . . was great." It took him a minute to get it all out between gasps.

Before I could react, he turned me over and pinned my hands over my head. "You're such a curious little thing."

"Just tell me."

He let out a noisy exhale. "Fine, I booked us a spa day for two."

He booked a what? Oh, holy heck.

"Elle, what's wrong?"

"Those are expensive. Most of what we've done or booked so far wasn't too bad and the costs of each thing sort of traded off."

He released my hands and rolled off to rest on his elbow. "I wanted to do this with you. It's my treat."

"And it's really sweet." I rolled to face him and held his hand. "I wasn't joking about how long I saved for this trip. I also watched the resort's website until I noticed a promotion. The company is doing well, but I came with a budget I need to stick to. I don't want to rely on you to make up the difference. I don't even want to think about how much today cost."

"It's a regular service of the resort. It probably wasn't as much as you think. Besides, I had the best day with you on that sandbank. I would've paid ten times the amount if someone said we could do it again." He wrapped his arm around me and pulled me closer. "I want to spend the rest of our vacation the way we did today—enjoying being together."

I laid my head on the bed and looked up at him. "Would you have booked a spa day if it weren't for me?"

"With the amount of stress I've been under lately? Definitely. You've just relieved most of it by spending time with me."

My hand cupped his cheek. "Do you want to talk about it?"

He pressed his lips to my palm before he gave a tiny shake of his head. "We'll talk about it, but not right now. I don't want to think about any of it until it's time to go home." He pulled me into an embrace and buried his face in my neck, teasing that spot that drove me crazy with his lips.

"Will you go with me tomorrow?"

"Yes." I'd follow him just about anywhere.

His hand slid up my leg and I lifted my knee, hoping to get closer—hoping that hand would travel where I so desperately wanted it. Soft lips traveled up my cheek until they caressed mine, each stroke deliberate and sensual. He shifted as I sat up and removed my crocheted swimsuit cover.

"This is very pretty on you. It's so delicate, like you are."

"My sister made it for me. I always have scarves, sweaters, gloves. If it can be crocheted, she can make it."

He took my cover and tossed it to the chair instead of the floor. I don't know how long we laid there and kissed before we reluctantly dressed and ventured out for food. After several days of room service Thai, we wanted something new.

We spent the night in my villa pretty much making love or sleeping. William made me feel things I'd never known possible. People say that a lot, and I suppose it is rather cliché, but it was the truth.

Everyone has self-confidence issues. I preferred to ignore that little whispering voice that tried to bring me down, but mine stopped when I was with William. In his eyes, I was beautiful and special, which when you grew up with a mother like mine was pretty damn fantastic. I reveled in his attention and tried to make sure I made him feel the same.

I walked away from the spa day more relaxed and happier than I can ever remember. I'd been massaged, had a facial, and William and I had this detoxifying mud treatment where we smeared different color muds all over each other. After, I'm surprised he didn't have to carry me back to my rooms. I felt like such a wet noodle. That night, I'm not sure why, but we ended up in his villa. We made love and talked and made love again until we fell asleep sometime after midnight.

When I woke the next morning, the shower was running, and from the lack of heat behind me, he was already getting cleaned up for the day. A buzzing noise came from his side of the bed, and I glanced over to where his phone vibrated on the nightstand.

I wrapped the sheet around me and started making myself coffee. About the time I turned on the coffee maker, the phone stopped rattling. While my much-needed cup of caffeine brewed, I walked onto the patio and leaned against one of the beams. The view had still not gotten old.

The buzzing started again and I looked over to his phone. Maybe I should answer it. What if it was an emergency? It still seemed a rather nosy thing to do so I turned my back on it and continued staring at the ocean. After almost a minute, I returned to pick up my cup and the darn cell phone started vibrating again.

Three times in succession had to be important. I picked up the phone, swiped the screen and put it to my ear. "Hello?" For someone so eager that they called three times in a row, it was curious that not a sound came through the line. "Hello? Is anyone there?"

"Who is this and why are you answering my husband's phone?"

Chapter 7

I froze and my heart dropped to my feet. His wife? That high I'd been riding for the last few days ended with an abrupt thud as I dropped to the bed.

"Are you still there? I'm waiting for an answer, you little whore."

It took a couple of tries to get anything out. "Housekeeping ma'am. I was cleaning the room and the phone wouldn't stop ringing. I thought it might be an emergency."

"Oh," she said rather quickly. "It's not an emergency, but I do need to speak with him. Could you give him the message?"

"I'll write it down, ma'am." My voice was almost a whisper it was so hoarse.

"Could you give me the name of this place?"

My eyebrows drew together. She didn't know where he was? Then, that angry voice from the day I arrived played in my head. *"How would you come here? You don't even know where I am."*

"I'm sorry ma'am. If he didn't tell you, then I'm not at liberty to say, but I'll pass along the message."

An overly loud sigh came through the phone. "I suppose that will do. Make sure you give it to him."

"Yes, ma'am. Have a nice day."

She must've hit end before I did because the phone cleared back to the lock screen, an image of William, his father, and his sister taken when she started Boston Conservatory. He'd shown it to me that day we shopped on the island. My hands shook—hell, my whole body was shaking. I was going to throw up. I stood, dragged in a deep breath, and blew it out right as the bathroom door opened.

"Good morning, beautiful." When William stepped out, he wore a huge smile that fell like lead was attached to the ends. "Good Lord, what is it? Are you okay?" He took two steps forward and made to wrap his arms around me, but I couldn't.

I pushed him back and held his phone between us. "You need to call your wife."

His fingers wrapped around the device as his eyes closed. "Elle, it's not what you think."

I quickly grabbed my clothes off the floor. "Why? Are you separated? Getting a divorce?"

"Not yet."

I sat on the bed and pulled on my bikini bottoms followed by my white shorts. "Not yet? Does she know this?" When I stood, I buttoned them up and grabbed my bikini top, fastened the back and pulled it over my head.

"The marriage has been over for a long time. You have to believe me."

When my bikini slipped over the sheet and covered my breasts, I pulled the bedding away. "How? How am I supposed to believe you?" I don't know how I didn't rip my top with how hard I shoved my arms through the sleeves. Pivoting around on my heel, I faced him head-on. "How am I supposed to believe anything you've told me?"

"I've always told you the truth! I know I didn't tell you about this, but I did try to walk away, remember?"

"And that's supposed to excuse everything? It's supposed to make it better?" I started to button up my blouse while I stared at him. "You said that if we wanted, when our vacations were over, that we'd make it work. Was that you coming to visit a weekend here and there and then going back to your wife and two point five children when you weren't with me?"

"No!" He dragged his fingers through his hair. "Before I came here, I fully intended to ask Claire for a divorce. I swear! And we don't have children. Claire would probably slit her wrists if she found out she was pregnant. I told you that I'd tell you everything before we left. Do you remember?"

"Do you think telling me then would've made a difference? This was something you should've explained to me before you fucked me. But I also screwed up. I should've made you tell me."

"Elle." His voice tugged at me, implored me to stop.

"Don't call me that." I practically growled the words. He had no right. He never did. As much as I wished he was, he wasn't mine.

"I've fallen in love with you."

I shook my head and covered the crown of my head with my hands. "No! No, no, no." I stood straight and pointed across the corner of the bed at him. "Whether it's true or not, that's not fair and you know it! How dare you!"

"It's true. I know you're scared to trust me, but if you'd let me explain everything. I can. I can make everything better. I'm going home to file for divorce. If I couldn't be with Claire before, I definitely can't now that I know what it's like to be with you."

A laugh that I didn't recognize came from me. This heavy chuckle that somehow paired itself with the tears blurring my vision. "I can't do this. I won't be the other woman. I *refuse* to be the other woman."

"You'd never be that. I swear!"

"How is that supposed to mean something?" A tear dropped to my cheek. "You claim you've been honest with me, but you conveniently forgot to tell me about your wife—a lie by omission, don't you think?"

"Please," he said. He took a small step forward, but I matched him by stepping back.

"No, I can't. I don't know how I'm supposed to believe anything that comes out of your mouth."

"I can prove myself to you."

I closed my eyes and took a deep breath. My cheeks were wet from the tears now dripping from my chin. "I don't know if I can . . ."

"Do you care for me?"

"That isn't fair."

"Elle—"

"I said not to call me that! That name was for the man I was falling in love with—the man I thought I'd started something incredible with—not for the man who actually belongs to someone else." A sob escaped, but I choked it back. I couldn't. Maybe when I was alone and I didn't have him trying to convince me to cave. This desperate little piece of my heart wanted to grasp the hope he offered and never let go, but I couldn't let that part rule me. I had to be practical. How many men strung along lovers while they pretended to be loving, doting husbands? I couldn't take that chance. If my heart was this shattered and splintered now, I might not survive if he did it again in six months or after a couple of years.

"I have to go." He held out his arm to stop me, but I turned to the side and bypassed it. "I have to go. I can't continue on like this." Grabbing my strappy sandals, I ran out to the pathway, and to my villa. Once I was inside, I shut and locked the door. I even closed up the sliding glass door on the patio just in case."

Once in private, I collapsed on the bed and sobbed and sobbed until I'd exhausted myself. I had to have wrenched every last tear from my body, and now, my eyes hurt like I'd been trying to blink sand out of them. When I sat up, I scanned everything around me. He was a part of this room. I would never be able to remain here without seeing him—standing in the shower with that sexy smile, lying on the lounge chair on the patio, sitting up against the headboard of the bed. Any other room at the resort likely would have the same problem. They were all too similar.

First, I'd have to see if I could swap my ticket for a last-minute flight out. Hopefully, it wouldn't put me into debt for the next year. A quick internet search on my phone provided the local phone number for the airline. I dialed for an outside line on the room's phone and let my imagination run wild, creating a family emergency. As it turned out, a couple of seats were available on the next flight and the lady could get me into one of them for no extra charge. The bad part was she could only get me as far as London before no more spare seats were available for grabs. London was still better than next door to William! He would make another attempt to speak to me if I stayed. I couldn't keep him from trying.

I glanced over to the clock. I had two hours to pack, get my butt to the airport, and make it through security. I'd already packed up most of my dirty clothes, which definitely made things easier. I took everything out of the dresser and threw it on my bed, barely folding it before I tossed it on top.

I'd need someone to come get my bags and a way to get to the airport. I grabbed the phone and dialed for the concierge.

"Hospitality, how may I help you?"

"Yes, I need to check out early due to a family emergency. I have a flight in about two hours. Will there be a boat out before then?"

"Yes, miss. The next service to the airport is in twenty minutes. Will you need a porter to collect your luggage?"

I glanced into the bathroom at my toiletries strewn across the vanity. "Yes, villa one-ten please."

"We'll have your bill ready for you when you come to the lodge."

"Thank you."

I hung up and began flying around the room, gathering my belongings. I put a spare outfit in my crochet bag. I didn't have time to change now, but I might on the flight. Changing in an airplane bathroom wasn't the most appealing option, but I wouldn't change planes until after a nine-hour flight to Rome. I really wanted something a bit warmer before I arrived in London. I'd never been to England, but it didn't take a genius to know the weather in November wouldn't be shorts and bikinis!

I made one last run through the villa after the porter arrived. He even followed behind me to make sure I hadn't forgotten anything. Then, he carried out my suitcase while I gathered my purse and my crochet bag, slinging it over my shoulder before I hurried after him.

Every part of me trembled. I didn't want to run into William. He'd try to stop me, and what if I couldn't say no? So far, I was proud of myself for standing up to him. I needed to hold my ground and not buckle.

Fortunately, I never caught a glimpse of him, and the front desk had me checked out in a matter of minutes. Afterward, I walked straight to the airport transfer service and settled in, sitting as far as possible from the other guests on board while I cried. And only an hour earlier I thought I was out of tears!

Security at the airport wasn't terrible. I even managed to get a decent cup of coffee before my flight. I bought a muffin, but it never came out of the bag. I hadn't eaten since last night, but I was more nauseated than hungry. I'd never handled stress well. It always made my shoulders ache and my stomach queasy.

Once I was on the plane, I realized the woman who worked for the airline squeezed me into first class. I didn't know how it happened, but who was I to argue? I had nine hours to kill, my phone battery was nearly dead, and my seat had this great USB port where I could plug it in. As soon as the flight attendant completed the pre-flight briefing, I put my earbuds in and tried to distract myself from thinking about William. Whether I would be successful or not remained to be seen!

Roughly fourteen hours later, I dragged myself into London Heathrow, exhausted and my heart physically hurting. I shouldn't have drunk the complimentary champagne or the wine that came with the meal I couldn't bring myself to eat. I nibbled on the bread, which did settle my stomach some, but not as much as I would've liked.

I'd used different airlines for the long trip, so now, I needed to find the counter for the next leg. I wasn't going to hold my breath, but I crossed my fingers and toes they had a seat available on a flight out tonight.

It took an hour to clear customs, find baggage claim, and wait for my luggage. I followed the signs to the main part of the terminal and found the desk for the airline, waiting another twenty minutes before I finally made it to the counter.

"Good evening." The woman, whose name tag said Millie, was entirely too happy.

I held out my travel packet. "Hi, I have this ticket, and I would like to see about getting it swapped for an earlier flight—preferably tonight."

She took the paper from me. "Let's see what we've got." After a series of clicks, she clucked her tongue and shook her head. "I'm very sorry. We're booked solid. I'm afraid our next flight out is the one you already have booked."

"What about anywhere in the U.S.?"

"All of our flights to the United States go into either Chicago, Newark, or Boston. I've checked every one that leaves between now and your existing flight. I'm sorry." She held up my ticket for three days from now. "You could try another airline, but I'm afraid your airfare is non-refundable."

I took my ticket and smiled as best I could. I checked the departure boards and inquired about one or two flights, but the fares were outrageous and most of them didn't have seats left. It would've been cheaper just to stay in London until I flew out again.

I made my decision and logged onto the airport Wi-Fi, hoping to find a reasonably priced place to stay. After a few duds, I clicked on a site for apartments near St. Paul's Cathedral priced less than a major hotel chain just around the corner. The idea of my own space appealed to me. I wouldn't have to socialize or put on a happy face when I left my rooms. I could pick up something to cook if I got hungry. Only a few clicks booked me into a flat, as they called it, but now, I had to figure out how to get there!

"Excuse me!" I called to what appeared to be a man from airport security as he passed. He turned, and I pasted on my best friendly smile. "Could you point me in the direction of the currency exchange, please?"

"They're closed by now, love. If you need money, there's a cash point just down the terminal on the left."

"A cash point?"

He gave a light chuckle. "Sorry, I believe your lot call it an ATM."

"Oh! I hate to think of the service charge on that one."

"What are you trying to do, if you don't mind me asking?" The man leaned in a little, though it wasn't intrusive. His greying hair and bushy eyebrows gave him this grandfatherly quality that wasn't threatening.

I breathed out. I needed to sleep—badly. "I can't get a flight out for three days, so I've found a place to stay near St. Paul's Cathedral. The problem is that I need to get there so I need cash for a taxi."

The man patted me on the arm. "Most taxis take credit cards, but you'll pay dearly for a trip into the city. If you want a quick and cheaper way to get there, I'd take the Heathrow

Express to Paddington Station then take the Bakerloo line to Oxford Circus, swap to the Central line and there'll be a tube stop for St. Paul's." He motioned her to follow. "Come with me. I'll show you. I don't have to be back on for another twenty minutes anyhow. Wait and go to a cash point tomorrow. There are a number of them around where you're staying."

"I don't mean to use up your break. I'm sorry."

"No worries." He walked me to the terminal, helped me buy an Oyster card—a declining balance card used to travel on the subways—from one of the machines, and gave me a map to the London Underground. Without his help, I wouldn't have known where I was going, but it turned out to be not as difficult as I would've thought. Navigating my suitcase in and out of the train was a bit of a pain. At least nothing was crowded at that time of night.

By the time I checked in and had the quick tour of my "flat," I locked the door, dropped onto the bed, and let out a sob. I don't remember much after that.

Chapter 8

Four days later, I stepped off the plane at Charleston International. If I'd said I felt better than I did when I arrived at Heathrow, I'd be lying my ass off. I wasn't quite as tired, but my chest still ached, though that was probably normal for someone who'd had their heart splintered, broken, and left in pieces in some remote part of the Indian Ocean. I not only hated that I was weak, but also that I cried at the worst times. On my second day in London, I saw a travel ad for Indonesia in the Underground, and I sobbed. William and I weren't even in Indonesia for crying out loud!

When I woke up on my first day in England, my first impulse was to burrow under the covers and wallow. It would've been so easy to do. I wouldn't have needed to shower and the apartment had brochures for several "takeaway" places that delivered. But while I drank my coffee, I shed enough tears to fill the Thames, so I put my foot down. I wouldn't do this to myself. I had to get out of those rooms and do something or I would've gone mad thinking of William.

That first day, I walked to St. Paul's and crossed Millennium Bridge. At that moment, I laid eyes upon my salvation—the Tate Modern. Instead of wandering aimlessly around London, I spent the next three days standing in front of great works of art that spoke to my soul. I sank myself in other people's emotions and misery in a vain attempt to forget mine just for a brief moment. After I saw everything in the Tate Modern, I went to the Tate Britain, the National Gallery, the

National Portrait Gallery, and I toured St. Paul's. If they possessed artwork, I was game.

"Ellie!"

I found Jena's golden blonde hair from all the way across the arrivals area. At five foot nine, my sister stood taller than most women and even some men, so her hair tended to be what I looked for in a crowd. We met each other half-way, and when she reached to hug me, I threw my arms around her and heaved in a breath as I tried not to cry.

"Ellie? What's wrong, honey?"

"I feel so stupid." I sniffed and pulled myself together, letting her go so I could wipe my eyes.

"I don't understand. You sent me a bunch of pictures about a week ago and told me everything was 'amazing.'"

"I promise to tell you everything, but can we get out of here first? I really don't want to turn into a blubbering mess in front of all these people."

Her long, silky tresses bounced when she nodded. "Of course. Let's get your bag. Are we going to need alcohol?"

"Normally, I would say yes, but I don't know if my stomach can handle it. The stress is tearing it up." I rubbed my hand across my belly. All day every day, since I left the island, I suffered from a lingering nausea. The wine on the flight to Rome was bad enough. I wasn't going to do that again!

"Okay, so no wine. We're going to need to go to the grocery store. Your fridge is empty."

I groaned. "I don't need food. Just leave me at home. I think I have some coffee in the pantry and an expired half gallon of milk left."

"Eww, no."

Yes, I was whiney, but I simply couldn't muster mature adult at the moment. The conveyor belt started moving, and I perked up. The sooner I got my bag, the sooner I could go home!

"There it is!" said Jena, as she spied the special tag she'd made me before the trip. The two of us hauled the suitcase off, and Jena led the way to the short-term parking where her little compact hybrid sat in one of the closest spaces.

Once we were driving away from the airport, I leaned my head against the glass and watched the familiar views pass until they blended into Marysville. Even though I protested, Jena insisted we stop and buy groceries. With a moderate amount of grumbling, I followed her inside and took the cart from her, ensuring we didn't spend the next hour wandering the aisles. By the time we returned to the car, she was the one grumbling while she carried two bags—and most of it was what she'd insisted I'd need.

When we pulled up to the curb of my building, I scrambled out faster than I had at the supermarket and pulled my suitcase from the backseat. I lived in an old building that had a gift shop on the first floor with a violently purple door to the one side of the shop window for access to the upstairs. I peeked into my mail slot when I stepped inside the hall, but it was empty.

"I came by on my way to the airport and put your mail in the kitchen."

"Thanks," I said, trudging up the stairs after Jena.

"You look like shit." At the different voice, I stopped, staring up the steps in front of me. Charlie stood at the top with her arms crossed over her chest.

"Just what I needed to hear." She always did have a way with words. "I love you too."

"I know."

"What are you doing here?" I said as I hugged her.

"Jena texted me when you were shopping and told me I needed to come over. She actually put 911 on it. I can see why."

I unlocked my door, steered my suitcase inside, and threw my keys onto the closest shelf. "You know she would've told you later anyway."

Jena shut the door behind her. "Not if you didn't want me to. Now, let's get a load of laundry on before we talk."

"Everything's clean. I washed it all before I left London."

They both gaped at me with wide eyes. "London?"

Charlie sat on the coffee table in front of me. "Okay, come on. Spill."

I covered my face with my hands and groaned. "You're going to think I'm an idiot."

"You know that's not true." My older sister sat beside me and grabbed my hand as I started to drop it to my lap.

I sucked in a deep breath, blew it out, and started from the beginning. I told them everything—well, not *exactly* everything. They didn't need to know some of it, only the important parts. Tears tracked down my face by the time I finished, and I couldn't look at my sister or my best friend. They would have some sort of lecture. I was hardly blameless. I should've seen the signs. I should've . . . I sniffed while I watched my fingernail scratch at a pull in my jeans.

"That fucker!" As I said, Charlie always did have a way with words.

"There has to be some explanation." My sister was ever the optimist. She always wanted people to be kind and good. Nothing was ever purposeful or malicious. One day, someone was going to hurt her badly. I hoped it wouldn't happen, but I didn't see how it was avoidable.

"What kind of explanation would be good enough?" Charlie glared at Jena. The fact that William was far, far away was a good thing, or else he might've been missing a vital part of his anatomy by the end of the evening. After breaking Jena's heart in eighth grade, Brian Crawford sported a swollen testicle for a week courtesy of Charlie—and all he'd done was tell her he wanted to break up. "*Even if* his marriage was truly over, he should've told Ellie from the beginning."

Jena squeezed my hand. "What if he does divorce his wife? What if he comes looking for you?"

I shrugged and leaned my head on her shoulder. "I don't know. I'd have to see how I feel when or if it happens. I know he'd have to earn back my trust. It would be impossible to pick up where we left off."

"Good answer," said Charlie. "Whether you took him back or not, you know I'd have to beat his ass first."

Jena threw up her hands and let them fall. "Jesus, Charlie! Maybe we shouldn't let you work with clients."

Charlie's hands flew to her hips. "Hey, you know I would never speak this way at work."

"Speaking of work, did anything exciting happen while I was away?" I glanced back and forth between them. Time to change the subject. Charlie never was all that eloquent, but she was right; she could speak and behave professionally when she needed to.

Charlie stood and grabbed a grocery bag we'd left forgotten. "The Taylor-Norton wedding was called off. I sent them an invoice on Wednesday."

I lifted my eyebrows and, no doubt, gaped. "They waited until two weeks before the big day to cancel?"

"As long as we get our fees, the bride can run away with the father of the groom for all I care," said Charlie while she unloaded and put the food away. "I signed a new client."

"I signed two." Jena hopped up and started helping Charlie. "It'll be another jam-packed June."

Lifting my feet, I sat sideways and laid my cheek on the back of the sofa. "It always is."

When they were done, my sister laid down my suitcase and unzipped it.

"You don't have to do that. I'll take care of it later."

"I don't mind, and you're practically falling asleep where you sit."

She had a point. "The sleep clothes on top are dirty. The rest is all clean."

Jena pulled out a pair of beaded strappy sandals and held them up. "These are new."

"And seriously cute!" Charlie snatched them from Jena and started to put them on. "Where did you get them?"

"The resort had several shops. William saw those and insisted on buying them for me."

Charlie's grin contorted. She pulled them off and tossed them back to Jena. "Those go on the burn pile."

"No," I choked out. I scurried to pick them up and put them in my closet. They both were looking at me when I turned around. "No." Charlie lifted her eyebrows to Jena.

"Don't do that. I don't want to see him, and it still hurts like someone ripped my heart out of my chest and used it for a trampoline, but I can't burn anything. I can't even bring myself to delete the photos of him on my phone.

"You haven't shown us what he looks like," said Charlie as she sat down next to me.

I pulled up the selfie we took the day of the sandbank picnic. When I tilted the phone, she snatched it from my hand.

"Woah! Hello, Clark Kent." She held the phone out so Jena could see.

My sister rolled her eyes dramatically. "You're crazy, Charlie. He doesn't even wear glasses."

"Slap a pair of nerdy glasses on the dude, and he would definitely be a Clark Kent. Doesn't matter which one—Henry Cavill, Tom Welling, or Christopher Reeve. They're all hot." I started to giggle at Charlie's silliness, and she hugged me tight and whispered in my ear. "You know we're here for you whenever you need us. It doesn't seem like it now, but it will get better."

"I love you."

Charlie wiped the tears from my face. "Love you too."

"Umm, Ellie?"

"Yeah," I said, turning to Jena.

"I don't mean to pry, but this isn't the box of condoms I packed in your bag."

My face burned like it had caught fire, and I bit my lip. "We sort of had to buy another box."

A huge gasp filled the quiet moment. "Ellie! That was a pack of twenty!" My best friend, sitting next to me, snorted and began to guffaw.

"Well, aren't you glad to know we practiced safe sex?" I crossed my arms over my chest and curled up a bit more. "And besides, several tore when we took them out."

"Not when you were using them?" While Jena's eyes bulged to the size of half-dollars, Charlie held her stomach while she continued to laugh.

"No! When we were taking them out of the package. We were sort of in a hurry."

Charlie reached forward and grabbed a tissue from the box on the coffee table.

Jena's eyes narrowed. "How many tore?"

I scratched the back of my neck. "I don't know. Maybe two."

"We don't have to ask if the sex was good." Charlie still chortled. "I'm surprised you didn't get off the plane permanently bow-legged."

Jena coughed and tossed the box onto the coffee table. "Well, at least we know there won't be any consequences."

I hugged the pillow to me tight. "I can't look at it. You do it."

Jena's eyes bulged to the size of saucers. "You want me to do it? It's for you. You should do it."

I started shaking my head so hard it throbbed.

"Oh, give me a break! I'll do it!" Charlie got up and walked into the bathroom, coming out two seconds later with the white stick in her hand. "It's positive."

I buried my face in the pillow, fell back onto my bed, and screamed. Next thing I knew, the pillow was pulled from my face, and Charlie loomed over me, her bobbed ginger hair hanging to one side.

"Do you know what you want to do?"

I gulped back the vomit that hadn't left its ever-present spot in the back of my throat—my lingering companion since the day I left the island. "What I want is for William to have been divorced all along and have him here with me, but I can't have that."

"You know what I mean," said Charlie dryly.

"I won't get rid of it. I can't." I pulled myself back up, still clutching the pillow to my middle.

"What about adoption?" Jena's voice held a soothing tone while she rubbed my back.

I covered my eyes with my hand and breathed in a futile attempt to settle my stomach. Could I give this baby up? Plenty of people wanted a baby desperately, but I loved William, even if he was a crap bag as Charlie had taken to calling him. I couldn't give away the only bit of him I had left. Adoption might be the unselfish thing to do, but giving up the child I had with William would kill me.

Shaking my head, I choked out, "I can't. I know what we had was wrong, but even after going over it a million times in my head, I do think he loved me. I'm probably being silly and naïve, but if I am, then so be it. I can't give it up. I hope you won't ask it of me."

"Of course not," said Jena. "I simply want you to be certain of your decision."

"I am." I was scared but I knew what I wanted.

"You have medical insurance through the company," chimed in Charlie. "You won't have to worry about that. And you have us for help."

"I know, but I do have a lot to work out." I looked around me with a sigh. "This apartment is expensive for its size. In order to save money, I'll need to find somewhere less costly to live."

Jena clasped her hands in front of her. "I have a solution for that."

"Okaaay." I lifted my eyebrows and leaned in her direction. "Let's hear it."

"It might be better if I show you." She glanced at my ragged sleepwear. "You should change."

Twenty minutes later, we stood in front of one of the larger homes in downtown Marysville, an enormous classic red brick home with white trim. A lop-sided "For Sale" sign dangled from the metal railing on the steps.

Charlie looked around me to Jena. "What's this?"

"Our new office." My sister rubbed her hands together and then held them pressed together to her chin.

"We can't afford this," I said, staring at Jena. She'd lost her mind. It was also entirely too big for us. Maybe in five to ten years, but we didn't have the clientele or the profits to justify such a large space yet.

Jena turned to me and grasped my hands. "But we can. This was Mr. Phillips' law offices remember? The downstairs is all fixed up for a business. We might want to paint some of the stained bookcases or take them out, but it's pretty much ready to go. Meanwhile, Mr. Phillips lived upstairs on the second floor where there's a really nice kitchen, a living area, and two bedrooms. There's also another bedroom and bathroom on the third floor."

I looked back at the house and squinted. My stomach was churning again, so I took a heavy inhale of fresh air. "That's all that's on the top floor? It looks bigger than that."

"There's a door from the balcony along the side to a small apartment on the backside of the house. That's what makes up the rest of the third floor. The garage has also been converted into a small house that's rented out." Jena watched us as she dropped her hands to her sides with a thud. "Don't you see! The three of us together pay more for rent than what the cost of the mortgage on this house would be and then there's the garage apartment. Ellie, you and I could live on the second and third floor and Charlie could have the apartment to the back. The garden behind it is amazing too. The best part is that you wouldn't have to worry about daycare unless you wanted to. We could all pitch in and help."

I turned my head to find Charlie watching me. "What do you think?" I asked. She was the numbers girl. She'd know if we could swing it.

Charlie pulled a flyer from the nearby box. She stared at it and bounced her head back and forth a little but never cracked a smile, even when she looked up at me. "*I'm* not changing diapers."

Chapter 9

About a week after I'd arrived home, William did try to call me. We'd all agreed that I wouldn't be answering phones for a while, so Charlie ended up taking it. She dutifully took a message, but then informed him, in no uncertain terms, that she knew exactly who he was followed by a precise description of where he could shove his phone call. She didn't mince words, and he apparently didn't say much more. The message simply read, "I need to speak with you. Please call me." He did leave a number, but I gave it to Jena. I told her to throw it away. He called twice more and left the same message. I never called him back.

After I found out I was pregnant, I discovered that Jena never did throw away William's phone number. She produced it, as if by magic, and insisted I needed to call him. She was adamant that he should know.

Instead, I turned into the world's biggest coward. What if his marriage wasn't really over? What if he still happily played house with his wife? How could I raise a child with a man I couldn't trust? Was it fair to this baby to be stuck in the middle? What if William didn't even want to be a father? We hadn't dated like a normal couple. We weren't divorced. I'd been the other woman.

I clicked off the screen on my phone, blocking that selfie of William and me from sight. I couldn't keep doing this. The hormones had been brutal. If I thought I cried when I left the island, it was nothing to what I could do if I felt the urge now. I couldn't and wouldn't wallow in sadness. It wasn't good for me or the baby.

Charlie walked through my office door and held up a large brown envelope. "You received a package from the sperm donor. Should I burn it?"

"What?" I held out my hand and turned the flat package around so I could read it. "What could he have to send to me?"

My free palm pressed against my belly and rubbed back and forth. According to Jena, I'd started doing that when I began showing. Now, nearly five months along, I probably lived with one hand plastered to my bump.

"Maybe you should call him." Jena was leaning against the door frame. "You know, tell him you're going to have his baby. See if he left his wife."

Charlie crossed her arms over her chest. "Leave her alone, Jena. It's her decision, and she's made it. You need to respect that. The loser doesn't deserve her or the child anyway."

I glanced between the two of them. "I'm going out. I don't want to read this here."

"You could always go upstairs," said Jena. We'd purchased the house downtown, and thirty days later, when the sale had closed, we'd moved. With the help of Charlie's brother and some of our other friends, the business was up and running there by the next month. The location was brilliant, and my rent was half of what I'd been paying for my almost studio. The best part was that we had two of Marysville's churches within a block—one was even directly across the street, which made local weddings so much easier. Of course, Marysville was only a tiny fraction of our business: we organized weddings all over the area. However, the location was still a plus!

I couldn't rip my eyes from the envelope in front of me. "I think I'll go to the park. I have my cell phone if you need me."

"Or if you need us," said Charlie. She hugged me and gave me a kiss on the cheek. "If he makes you cry again, I might just have to track down the son of a bitch and kill him."

After I rolled my eyes, Jena hugged me too. They both wanted the best for me and wanted me to make the right decision, but it was funny how different their perceptions of what was best were.

The spring weather was still a bit cool so I grabbed my sweater, or "cardie," as the salesgirl in London called it, and pulled it on. I couldn't button it anymore, but it covered my arms instead of my maxi dress leaving them bare. It fit me a bit differently now than it did before the bump, but I loved it because it was soft and comfy, and even though it didn't cover my stomach, it still looked cute.

The park wrapped around the back of the church across the street so, within a matter of a minute, I walked down the familiar path towards the pond. I sat on a bench overlooking the water and blew out a noisy breath. A part of me wanted to throw the envelope in the lake, but I couldn't. I owed it to the baby to see what it said. Well, that's at least what I told myself. Another part of me was horribly curious.

My fingers shook as I pinched open the metal clasp and tore the flap, peeking inside before I pulled out a stack of papers with a handwritten letter paper-clipped to the top. I leaned back, closed my eyes, and just breathed for a moment. I needed to stop trembling. After a few minutes, I'd managed to gather my courage, open my eyes, and become entranced by the words in front of me.

Dearest Ellie,

I've tried to call, but I didn't want to force myself on you, and after my conversation with your friend Charlie, I thought it best to give you time. I have so much I need to tell you. I can only hope you read this letter.

Please know that I didn't lie to you that morning when I said my marriage was over. I don't know if you remember the conversation, but I once told you that after my mother's death, I went through a sort of self-destructive phase. I met Claire during that time. While some families might draw together after the death of a loved one, my father and I didn't get along. He hated Claire, so to annoy him, I kept dating her. I never intended to marry her, but after one drunken night in Vegas, I woke up married according to the certificate on the bedside table. That was four years ago.

For the first year, we got along fine. Our relationship wasn't what I'd always dreamed of, but it was what I had. I felt obligated to try. After that, our marriage slowly deteriorated. My wife became more interested in almost everything but our marriage—shopping, going to the local wine bar with her friends, the spa. She became like one of those women in that Housewives reality television show, and the more she changed, the unhappier I became.

During this time, my father and I repaired our relationship and became very close. I'd never spoken badly about Claire, but almost a month before I met you, he informed me that he believed Claire to be cheating. He had no proof but had heard rumors around town. My wife and I were never intimate anymore—we hadn't been for a long time. I admit to being relieved at his suspicions. I had an easy way out if she was unfaithful.

My father and I hired a private investigator and booked my trip to the island. Claire called me once when I arrived, which I found strange, but I'd told her I was going away on vacation on my own. I think she was more annoyed that I went somewhere she might want to visit more than me leaving. According to the private investigator, she waited all of two hours before she met a man at a hotel across town. While I was away, not only did she go there, but he came to my house almost as much as she went to him.

I have no idea why she called that morning when you answered the phone—unless in the back of her mind she'd thought I'd found someone else. She didn't know where I'd gone, since I'd only given my father my travel itinerary and no one else. She probably played a hunch.

I wasn't lying when I said my marriage had been over for a long time. I can't remember the last time we'd had sex, and we never spent time together. If I'm being honest, I never loved her—and I know that now because what I feel for you is so much more than I ever thought possible. It's a part of every fiber of my being. I can't just unwind it and forget about it, not without tremendous pain.

You don't trust me. I do understand why. I should've told you from the beginning. I warred with myself about what I was doing spending so much time with you when I was so attracted to you. My internal struggle only became worse the more we were together. I started to have feelings, and that first night we kissed, I wanted you so badly but needed to do what was right. Of course, I failed spectacularly at that.

My father had emailed me a few days before Claire's call to let me know she'd been photographed with a man. I became extremely angry. For all those years, I'd tried desperately to be a decent husband. I'd lost so much time to that sham of a marriage, and while I watched you talk to Rob, I felt I was losing you too—all because of some crazy, mistaken loyalty to Claire. When we arrived back at the resort, I decided to forget about all of it and grasp what I wanted for the first time in forever. The urge was selfish. I admit it. As far as I was concerned, my marriage existed only on paper. In every other way, it was dead. I only had to bury it.

I called after I returned home to tell you I'd filed for divorce. I hoped then as I do now that you might be willing to start again—to learn to trust me once more. I live in Savannah, so I'm not too far from you. We have construction projects in both Georgia and South Carolina. I can work from there just as easily as I can from here. My father has even offered to oversee any projects in Georgia so I can move closer to you. I want us to be together. That is, if you can find it in your heart to forgive me—if you love me as I love you.

I know I need to earn your trust back. Because of that, I do have to tell you that Claire is contesting the divorce. With the financial agreement she signed when we returned from Las Vegas, my attorney claims she doesn't have a leg to stand on, but it's delayed matters far longer than I would like. I've enclosed a copy of my separation papers as proof that I'm not hiding anything from you. I can also introduce you to my attorney if it's necessary. I just want you, if you can forgive me, to give me a second chance. My business card with my work number is

attached and I've included my cell phone number. Please call
me. I desperately need to hear your voice.
Love,
William

My cheeks were soaked when I reached his signature. I had damp patches on my dress where the cardigan was open in the front. He was getting a divorce. Based on what he'd written, he would've divorced his wife whether he'd met me or not. We could start over if I wanted. I started to shake. I'd had dreams where he came for me, told me he'd divorced, and swore he desired no one but me. Was that going to happen for real? Could we be together?

Picking up the corner of my sweater, I wiped as much of the damp from my face as I could. Why hadn't I brought a tissue? The entire box wouldn't be enough, my cheeks were so wet.

"Excuse me, ma'am, but are you okay?"

My hand flew to my chest and I inhaled sharply.

"I'm sorry if I startled you." The man standing in front of me smiled warmly. He was good looking, just under six feet with sandy blonde hair and brown eyes. He was no William, though.

"It's fine." I bent the papers over in front of me so he couldn't read them. "I'm fine. Thank you. Hormones, you know?" I rubbed my hand over the bump. "They get worse and worse."

"Oh! No problem. I did want to make sure you weren't hurt."

"I appreciate that."

94

He looked down and his brow furrowed. "Davies Construction? Are you considering them for a project?"

What? I peered down. The return address on the envelope! Now, how on Earth was I supposed to answer? He'd gone a little beyond good Samaritan with the question. "I—"

"Sorry." He laughed and combed his hair back from his face with his fingers. "I used to work for the company so I'm being overly curious. It's none of my business."

"You worked for them?"

"Yes, Grant Davies hired me just out of high school. I didn't have the money for college so I hoped to save up while I took a night class here or there so I was still gaining credit."

"That's a good idea."

"It was great until his son took over. It took me longer than I'd thought, you see, to save what I'd need with having to pay rent and bills. William Davies fired me, and for no good reason. Just said he didn't like me."

My eyebrows lifted. It didn't seem like the William I knew, but then I didn't really know him, did I? He didn't tell me about his wife. Maybe he treated me the way he did because he wanted something from me. "Did you see about getting your job back? There had to be something you could do legally."

"I didn't want to spend money on a lawyer when I needed to save for school. Besides, after the way he treated me, I didn't want to work for him anymore." He pointed his finger at me. "I'll tell you the person I feel the sorriest for is his wife."

"His wife?" Something inside me froze.

"That one is a really genteel lady. She was always out volunteering in the community. If it was a particularly hot day, she would bring us ice-cold drinks to the job site. My parents knew her from church. She was there every Sunday, but they never met the husband. From what my parents told me, he never went with her. The few times I saw them together, he behaved very rudely towards her too."

"I wonder why she stayed?" I said out loud but to myself.

"I've often wondered that myself."

A hip-hop song suddenly blared from somewhere and I jumped.

"Sorry about that." He reached in his pocket and took out his cell phone. "Speak of the devil. It's my mom. It's been nice talking to you."

"You, too." I held up my hand as he answered the call and walked away.

I dropped my head into my hands. How did I get myself into this? As I'd finished William's letter, something had stirred in my chest. I couldn't wait to dial that number and hear his voice, but now, I had doubts. What were the odds that someone would happen to know him here? Was his business bigger than I assumed? He worked in both states and Savannah wasn't that far from the South Carolina state line. It made sense that he would do business here as well.

"It's too much," I whispered. All of it. His wife, his divorce, and now this guy and his claims. It was more than I could deal with. I had to banish my worrying for the sake of the baby. As much as I loved William and missed him, I wanted all of the heartache and uncertainty to go away, and there was one way to do that—I had to leave William behind. My heart would heal, I could move on, and I wouldn't have any more of this crap to agonize over. Whether I wanted to or not, I had to. I had no choice.

Chapter 10

When I shut the door behind me, Jena and Charlie came out of their offices and leaned against their doorframes. It was rather funny seeing at them mirrored in almost identical poses, but I couldn't bring myself to smile. My heart hurt like that day I stepped off the plane at Heathrow. All I wanted was to curl into a ball under the covers and block out the world.

"Son of a bitch," said Charlie. "We shouldn't have given you the envelope."

"It wasn't what he sent that's bothering me. It's . . . complicated."

Jena waved me forward. "Come on, get in here. Tell us what's happened, and we'll see if we can't fix it."

Charlie followed me inside, and I sat down while the two of them leaned against the front of Jena's desk. "So, what did the asshole have to say?"

"He sent me this." I handed the two of them the letter as well as the copy of the legal paperwork. Charlie's eyebrows lifted when she looked over the paperwork, then she and Jena traded.

"I don't get it," said Jena. "This appears to be everything you could ever want. I feel terrible for the guy. He was stuck in a bad marriage, and while trying to arrange his divorce, he meets and falls in love with you. Then he loses you because he didn't tell you everything. You can't tell me even the tiniest little portion of your heart hasn't hoped he would walk through the door and sweep you off your feet."

"Of course I've felt that way, but that's not everything. I can't get caught up in the romantic when there's so much more to consider."

"What do you mean?" Charlie sat in the chair beside me and leaned on the arm so she was close while she watched me. "He sent you a letter explaining what happened and asked you to call. He's willing to work to earn back your trust. What's holding you back? Are you afraid he'll react badly about the baby? If he does, then he's an even bigger dick than I originally thought."

I shook my head and crossed my arms over my chest. "I don't know how he would react. I have a feeling . . . I mean, I hope he would be happy. It's what happened after I read the letter that has me concerned."

"I don't understand," said Jena. "What happened?"

"This man came up to me and asked me if I was okay. I told him I was, but before he left, he saw the return address on the envelope—I'd set it next to me on the bench. Anyway, he told me he worked for William's company. He was originally hired by William's father, but when William took over, he fired this guy simply because he didn't like him."

My sister's voice had that drawl she used when she disapproved. "You know as well as I do that he couldn't fire him without reason."

"Then why would the guy say it? He also said he knew William's wife and how amazing she is. She volunteers all of the time and she goes to church every Sunday and he told me how William never goes with her."

"I don't know, Ellie." She might have been talking to me, but Charlie's eyes looked to Jena. "I think I agree with Jena on this. You don't know this man. What if he was fired for a good reason? He might hold a grudge against William for it. I also find it really weird that this guy just happened to run into you in the park."

With a huff, I let my arms fall. "It's a small world. William is a good example of that! We live about three hours from one another, yet we meet on the other side of the world at a tropical resort because our villas were practically next door to each other."

I stood up and started pacing. "How do I know the William I fell in love with is the real one? It killed me when I found out about his wife, and I'd only known him for about ten days. I couldn't handle it if we started seeing each other again, and everything imploded months down the line. I wouldn't survive it. It was all I could do in London to get out of bed and drag myself out of that flat." The tears started to blur my vision, and Jena handed me the box of tissues from her desk. "That first day, I walked, almost in a trance, past St. Paul's and down to Millennium Bridge. It was cloudy, cold, and dreary, but I didn't feel the cold. I was that numb. It wasn't until I caught sight of Tate Modern that I came out of that daze. I can't do that again. I have to think of this child—my child."

"His child too," said Jena.

"What if we're better off without him?" I bit my lip and looked back and forth between them.

Charlie came over and hugged me. When she drew back, her hands stayed on my arms. "We can't make you do what we think is right. You have to decide what that is for yourself, but you have to be certain this is the right choice. Before I read that letter and saw the paperwork he included, I agreed with you. He didn't deserve you or this baby, but I'm not so sure anymore. What if he made a mistake? He's human, just like you are. He may have paid just as dearly for it as you have.

"Honey, you're one of the bravest people I know," said Charlie. "When you thought William might be married forever, you decided to keep the baby and raise him or her on your own. That takes guts, but so does fighting for what you want and taking chances."

"She's right." Jena stepped closer and took my hand. "You don't have to make the decision right this minute, but you need to do something soon."

"I can't." They didn't know how hard it was. Jena had dated in high school and had short relationships since then, but nothing like what I'd had with William. Charlie probably did understand a little. She'd had one long term relationship with her high school sweetheart and had lived like a nun ever since. "I know you're trying to help and I appreciate it, but he broke my heart. I trusted him and I don't know if I can bring myself to trust him with my heart again. Please, you have to let me work this out on my own."

My sister sighed. "You know we always have your back. We just don't want you to have regrets."

"Too bad you can't drink." Charlie smiled. "We could have one of our girls' nights."

"We don't have to have alcohol to have a fun evening," said Jena. "We can order pizza, we can always make virgin daiquiris or margaritas, and watch movies or play a game."

Charlie groaned. "I'll be working out for a week to get that off."

Jena waved off Charlie's complaining. "Well, the doctor did say Ellie should gain some weight. That morning sickness really kicked your butt. We need to pack on a few pounds for the baby."

I hugged my sister. "I could really go for some Ben & Jerry's Cherry Garcia. It's all I've been able to think about for days."

"Charlie," said Jena with some authority. "You're on groceries. We need ingredients for drinks and some Cherry Garcia. I'll order the pizza," she squeezed my hand, "unless someone has a craving for something different."

I bit my lip and glanced back and forth between them. "Burgers and fries from The Depot?"

"Oh, I agree." Charlie's eyes lit. "Would you be upset with me if I drank a beer?"

"If you two want wine or beer then drink what you want. I don't need any non-alcoholic mixed drinks. You could always pick up an Izze for me to drink. I hardly ever drink sodas so it would be a treat."

"I can do that." Charlie leaned around me to look at the clock on the wall. "We're almost done for the day, so if y'all don't mind, I'll go to the store. Jena, call in the order for the food, and I'll pick it up on my way back."

"Sounds good to me," said Jena.

"Me too." I sniffed and shoved my hands in the pockets of my dress. "I'm going to go wash my face."

I trudged upstairs to my room. When we'd first looked at the property, Jena and I loved the layout for our living area. She and I both had our own rooms and bathroom, mine with a set of French doors that connected my bedroom to an adjoining room, which was perfect for the baby. Jena's bedroom and bathroom were upstairs.

The original kitchen downstairs was larger, but Mr. Philips had put in a well-designed kitchen upstairs. It was small but made the use of the space it had very well and left the downstairs facilities free in the event a reception became booked for the back garden. It wasn't an idea we'd originally considered, but one of our clients knew how picturesque the courtyard and garden could be and requested it as the venue for her wedding and reception. We'd thought of it as a location for photos but not for a small, intimate wedding—especially since the flowers varied and bloomed from the azaleas in March until the potted mums we intended to spread around in October.

I placed my hands along the front of the vanity and leaned, inhaling heavily. The mirror reflected back exactly what I expected to see: puffy, red eyes, swollen nose, and dark circles and trails down my cheeks from my mascara running. Lovely, just lovely!

Once I'd removed my eye makeup and scrubbed my face, I dropped onto my bed and curled onto my side, unlocking my phone and opening my photo app. I brought up the photo of William and me on the sandbank. It was my favorite photo of us. We were so happy.

My heart ached from being tugged in so many different directions. I so wanted to ignore the man in the park and call William, but why would the stranger lie? What would he have to gain from it? He didn't know me. He also didn't know that my baby was William's.

I also had to think about the baby. What was best for him or her? Yes, it was usually better for a child to have both parents, but what if William was a liar and cruel to his employees? My child would be better off without him in that case.

"I locked up and brought the business phone upstairs." The hand holding my cell phone rested on the bed so I could see Jena. "We didn't have any other appointments today and it's twenty minutes before closing time. I don't think it's a problem."

She walked inside and laid down across the foot of the bed so we were face to face. "Do you feel okay?"

"I'm tired, but other than that, I feel fine. I think it's mostly from crying." The baby rolled in my tummy, and I rested my hand on that side.

"Is he moving?"

I nodded and took her hand, placing it where mine had been and pressing in a bit. The baby jabbed at Jena's fingers when they touched through my skin.

"Oh, Ellie!" she gasped. "Was that a kick or an elbow?"

"I don't know."

She lightened up her touch but left her hand with mine covering it. "When did you start being able to feel him like this?"

"This past week. At first, it was little pokes and rolls, but they've become more pronounced." I smiled at her. "You think it's a boy?"

"I don't know. If only he hadn't sat on his feet whenever you had your ultrasound, we'd know for sure. He's just so stubborn that he has to be a boy, but then, you're pretty hard-headed. It could be a girl too."

"Ha, ha."

"When's dad coming to paint the baby's room?"

Dad had been great since I'd told him. He painted my room and my bathroom when we moved in and helped Jena with the rest of the house. He insisted I shouldn't work too hard. Of course, those were the days I felt like I would never get up off the bathroom floor. I had such terrible morning sickness. I never argued with him.

"Next weekend."

"Did you decide on colors?"

I laughed and sat up so I could see in the room next to mine. "I found an idea on Pinterest. The walls will be painted grey to match my room."

"That'll look nice with the white trim."

"It'll also be easy to add some color when we finally find out what this little one is." My stomach growled.

Jena giggled and rubbed the side of my belly. "I think the little one is hungry."

"Starved."

My sister sat up and brushed her hair back from her face. "Do you think I'm wrong about it being a boy?"

I peered down to the bump and smoothed my dress over it. "I really don't know. I keep having this dream about a little girl with William's curls and brilliant blue eyes."

"You've never told me about that."

"They only started about a month ago. They aren't nightmares or anything detailed. Usually, we're playing in the park or I'm reading her a bedtime story."

"*The Poky Little Puppy?*"

I laughed at my sister's perspicacity. "You know it."

"Do you have any ideas for names yet?"

"I'm not sure. I'll probably need to buy a name book and go through it."

"That seems like a good idea. You can mark pages and highlight the ones you like that way. Maybe you can find some names online." Jena scooted to the edge of the mattress. "I want to throw on some pajamas. If we're going to stuff ourselves on burgers and ice cream, I want to be comfy."

"That's a good idea, but I don't want to get up."

"Come on!" She grabbed my hands and hauled me off the bed. "Get changed. Charlie will be back soon, and we have some serious girl stuff to do. We should have pedicure parties when you're further along and can't see your feet. We can paint your toenails."

I lifted one of my eyebrows. "Do you think Charlie would want to touch my feet?"

Jena snorted and rolled her eyes. "Good point. I don't think she even likes touching her own."

"I'm back!" came Charlie's yell from downstairs. "I hope you have everything ready because I've been smelling the burgers for the last five minutes and I'm hungry."

Jena hurried out, and I took my night clothes from the hook on my bathroom door and put them on. The bottom button on the top wouldn't close, but at least the bottoms were baggy and fit under my bump. I might be able to get through the pregnancy without having to buy new ones. Slipping on my fuzzy slippers, I headed out to the kitchen. For a moment I just stood by the door to watch Charlie and Jena unloading the food and listen to their happy banter.

I was really a lucky girl, with an amazing sister and a great best friend who stood by me no matter what. They would be there for the baby too. Was it all we needed? Maybe not for forever, but it'd definitely do for now.

Chapter 11

The next few months dragged by until I wanted to throw a temper tantrum of massive proportions. The bump grew and grew as June melted into July and the weather became hotter and hotter and hotter. In that southern summer heat, the baby made me boil from the inside out. Charlie became so tired of my griping that even though we had ceiling fans in nearly every room, she bought me a table top fan for my office, one for the living room, and one for my bedroom. At the same time, Jena complained I kept the house and office like a meat locker. I didn't see a problem. I was comfortable and neither of them were turning blue. It was a win-win. If they were so cold, they could always put on sweaters. I'd been dying for the baby to finally come and relieve my misery. I'd forgotten that you should always be careful about what you wish for.

I bent over, gripped the table along the wall, and breathed. The contractions weren't close enough together to wake up Jena or Charlie yet. They wouldn't mind if I disturbed them, but it was three in the morning. I'd let them sleep until I couldn't manage on my own or gritting my teeth stopped working and I screamed. They'd have no choice if it was the latter.

When the pain and tightness subsided, I started to walk around the house again. I'd already cleaned the kitchen and added what I wanted to my bag for the hospital. Jena would kill me if I tried to clean bathrooms or dust the light fixtures. I made an attempt a week ago, and my sister hadn't stopped lecturing me since.

Later, when the contractions prevented me from sleeping, I walked back into the living room where I turned on a lamp and sat in my favorite chair. One of the maternity photos I'd had taken caught my eye. Charlie insisted it needed a frame and a place outside of a photo album or scrapbook, a place where people would see it, which was why it was on the end table.

Micah, one of our friends from high school, now a local photographer, had offered to take the photos as a thank you for all of the wedding business we sent his way. That day, Jena and Charlie spruced me up, and he chauffeured me around to several locales for pictures. We'd started that morning, and driven all over, finally bringing me out to the beach just in time for a glorious sunset, which was the background for this particular photo.

I hadn't been too sure about the beach. Too many memories surfaced by merely driving past, but once we were out there on the sand, something seemed oddly right about it. I relaxed, and Micah had caught the picture perfectly. It was just dark enough that I stood in silhouette with the oranges, reds, and purples of the setting sun and the water as a postcard-worthy backdrop. The little sundress I wore stopped just above my knees, and I held a shawl behind me. I'd worn a hat for some of the photos, but in this one, my hair flowed freely down my back.

Air hissed through my teeth as I inhaled on the next pain. I pressed the home button on my phone. It'd only been six minutes that time. "Holy cow." My head dropped back and I closed my eyes to breathe through the worst of it. While my stomach tightened, trying to squeeze me to death, I focused on my breathing. When would this thing end? It had to be almost ten minutes already! The pain began to subside, and I panted.

Why was I out of breath? Had I held it? I really didn't know anymore.

Maybe it was time to wake Jena? By the time she dressed, the contractions would be at least five minutes apart, which was when the doctor said I should go to the hospital.

I waddled up the stairs and opened Jena's door, making her startle and sit up. "What's wrong?" Her voice was a bit hoarse but that was probably from being frightened awake. "Is it the baby?"

"Yeah, I think he wants to come out and he's getting pretty impatient."

Jena swung her legs over the side of the bed. "How impatient?"

"The last contractions were six minutes apart, but they've been steady since I've been awake."

She'd started walking toward the bathroom, but her steps came to an abrupt halt. "When did you wake up?"

"The first time was at eleven. When another contraction woke me up ten minutes later, I started walking around the house."

"You should've come to get me." Her tone was scolding. I knew she wouldn't like it.

"What good would it have done for you to be up all night too? I did sit and doze here and there, but I haven't been able to get comfortable and really sleep since midnight. I figured I could handle it on my own, and the two of you should sleep while you could."

"Have you tried waking Charlie yet?"

"God, no! You know how she is."

Jena picked up her phone and pressed the screen a few times. The line rang for both of them to hear until, "It better be time or I'm going to kick someone's ass."

The next wave hit. I doubled over, holding the footboard of Jena's bed. "Son of a bitch!"

"I'm up!" said Charlie. "I'll be down in less than five minutes. Don't go anywhere without me!"

I'd never seen those two get ready so quickly, but I've also never seen Jena leave the house without makeup. That girl could be puking her guts out and need to go to the ER, and she'd still have a flawless face. I was, however, willing to bet my child's non-existent college fund that Jena's entire cosmetics bag was in her purse.

Charlie's heavy foot was a godsend. I don't think I've ever made it to that side of town so fast in my life. Thank heavens the pain distracted me from her driving—even my clean-mouthed sister cursed during the ride. I was too preoccupied with breathing through a contraction to notice, but it had to be bad if Jena swore.

Fortunately, the nurses checked me in quickly, so instead of walking around the house, I paced around my hospital room while Jena put on her makeup and Charlie watched me like I was a sporting event.

"Are you sure you don't want that epi thing?" asked Charlie. "If I were in your place, I would offer them a million dollars for one."

I shook my head and breathed as steadily as I could through the unbearable pinch. "No, I want to be able to feel my feet. Besides, walking helps labor go faster."

"I'm going to miss the bump," said Jena in a wistful voice.

I straightened and looked at her. The woman was certifiably insane. "Then it's a good thing you didn't have to carry it. You can have the raw thighs from heat rash, the sizzling from the inside out . . . oh, and the swollen feet. I'd gladly give them all to you."

Jena looked at my figure like it was a dress she desired in a shop window. "But you carry it so well. You've glowed the entire pregnancy. You only really gained weight in your tummy. Not all women can claim that."

"No, my thighs and everywhere else also grew. Trust me on that. You didn't have to buy new panties because the old ones pinched your legs. My boobs also grew two cup sizes. I'm kind of scared of what's going to happen when my milk comes in."

Charlie snickered. "If those things get any bigger, you're going to fall over from being top heavy."

"Shut up," I growled. She wasn't intimidated. The little hussy only laughed harder.

I took a step and grabbed my belly with the hand not holding my IV tower, bending at the waist. "Fuck me!" Something warm trickled down my leg and started creating a puddle at my feet.

"You didn't have to pee in your pants." At that, my best friend cracked up laughing at her own joke. One day, she was going to have a baby and I'd be there. I might have to bide my time, but she'd pay.

"Seriously, Charlie?" Jena strode over and called for the nurse.

The woman bustled in, took one look at me, and helped me into the bed once the pain subsided, hooking me back to the monitors. "Let's see how things are going." She snapped on a glove and I closed my eyes and clenched my teeth while she probed around down there.

"Breathe, Ellie." My hand probably squeezed every last drop of blood out of Jena's before the woman stopped torturing me.

She ripped the glove from her hand and put it in the receptacle. "Have you felt like pushing yet?"

"No." I tensed and squeezed my eyes shut as another pain shot through my stomach and pelvis.

The nurse checked the tape coming from the machine at my side. "I'm going to go call the doctor. You're almost there. Good job, Mom."

"Forgive me if I don't high five you at the moment." The nurse laughed and hurried out.

"Almost there? What does that mean?" I opened my eyes as Charlie looked between me and Jena.

I shifted, trying to find a comfortable position. "How am I supposed to know? I don't do this every day."

Jena passed my hand to Charlie and disappeared into the bathroom. I panted through the rest of the contraction while Charlie brushed a few strands of hair from my face.

"Are you sure you don't want to call William?"

I nodded and squirmed in a useless attempt to ease the ache in my back and hips. "I'm going to do this on my own. I can do it."

"I know you can, sweetie, but I want to make sure you don't regret anything. It's your choice, and you know I won't go behind your back, but this baby should have a father."

Another contraction hit, and I made this high-pitched sound I don't think I could ever repeat if I tried. "I could get married one day and then there would be a father."

Charlie shook her head. "You'd have to fall in love with someone else, Ellie. Every day, you go through the motions of life, but you still love him and you miss him. All you're doing is coping."

"It's going to take time." I could get over him. I would get over him!

"It's been nine months."

"Charlie, please. It has to be this way. Besides, I don't see you running out and meeting anyone. Isn't this a bit hypocritical?" I dropped my head back onto the pillow and covered my eyes, pressing my lips together hard.

The bathroom door opened, and Jena returned. "You're having another one?"

"I need to push."

My sister rushed to the door while Charlie put her hands on my cheeks. "Look at me. Pant through it like they taught you in that class. Don't push yet. I'm not a doctor. I'll throw up instead of catching her."

My laugh came out kind of shrill and strangled. "You'd better not drop my baby."

The next thing I knew, my doctor was at my feet while two nurses took the foot off the bed and pulled out stirrups. "I hear you feel like pushing." She put on gloves and her hands disappeared under the covers. "Good timing. I'd just walked through the door for rounds." Was it good timing? Maybe the coincidence was a lucky one. I was too preoccupied at that moment to really give it much thought.

"Ellie," said Charlie through gritted teeth, "that's my fingers you're about to squeeze off."

"Ellie." Dr. Reynolds put her hand on my knee, drawing my eyes to hers. "You're ready to go. If you still feel the need to push, go for it."

This was it! I'd finally meet the little person I'd been growing inside me—all ten fingers and all ten toes of her . . . or him. I bore down with what energy I had left. Everything around me disappeared into a haze of noise I couldn't make out. It hurt. God, it hurt! Then, just when I thought the pain would last forever, it finally ended. I collapsed back onto someone. When I looked up, Jena kissed my hairline.

"You're doing amazing." The words may have been whispered near my ear, but I didn't miss them. "Look, they put up a mirror. You can watch if you want."

I had the hardest time keeping my eyes from closing, but I forced them open so I could see what the doctor could. Hopefully, Charlie didn't peek. All it would take was her catching sight of that and she'd hit the floor.

The muscles in my stomach started to tighten again, and I took a deep breath and forced myself to do it all over again. I lost track of how long and how many times I pushed. Jena whispered words of encouragement throughout, and Charlie ordered me to squeeze her hand as hard as I could then complained that it hurt.

All I remember is suddenly being relieved of that overwhelming pressure and having this squirming and squalling bundle placed on my chest. "Oh!" The nurse began wiping while the baby screamed. It was the most incredible sound in the world.

"Congratulations!" said the doctor over the din. "You have a beautiful baby girl!"

My vision blurred as tears began to fall. Like I didn't cry enough while I was pregnant! Before I was ready to let go of her, the nurse took her over to the warmer against the wall. I pushed Jena to follow. "Make sure she's okay? Please."

Jena grinned and gave me a thumbs up while my baby was checked over. My sister was also the one who brought her back to me once she was all cleaned and bundled. Until that moment, I hadn't noticed that Jena was crying too. "She's so sweet."

I wiped my eyes just before Jena placed her in my arms. I had a baby girl—a daughter. "Hello, sweet pea," I said, crooning. My finger traced her little forehead and the line of her nose. She resembled my newborn photos. My dad would love it.

"She's only six pounds two ounces, but she's definitely got a set of lungs." When I glanced up, the nurse shifted the blanket away from her face. "If you want to try breastfeeding, I can call a lactation consultant to help you."

"Thank you. Yes, I would."

When everyone finally cleared from the room, Charlie dropped into a nearby chair. "Holy shit, that was intense."

"That's it?" Jena had her hands out at her sides. "That's all you can think to say?"

Rolling her eyes, Charlie looked at me. "She's cute as . . . a bug. Okay?"

"Thank you," I said, grinning.

Charlie crossed her arms over her chest with a pout. "Do I really have to stop swearing?"

I laughed at her whining tone. "I know she can't say them now, but one day, she'll start mimicking what she hears. Could you imagine the old ladies at church if she said 'shit' at the age of two?"

"Might be kind of cute," said Charlie with a sly lift to one side of her lips.

The baby squirmed, and when I looked down at her, her eyes opened just enough to make out a pair of crystal blue irises before they fluttered closed again. I gasped.

"What is it?"

"Her eyes. They're William's."

Jena kissed my temple as she sort of half-sat on the bed. "Did you ever decide on a name?"

I'd hemmed and hawed over it to the two of them, but really, I'd known what I'd wanted to name a girl for months. "Freya. Freya Elizabeth."

Part 2

Chapter 12

I woke with a start, gasping for breath. I looked around the room and rubbed my face with my hands as I tried to breathe through my heart racing furiously in my chest. I hated that dream! I was back on the island, snorkeling with William, and he'd disappeared. I searched for him everywhere but couldn't find him. While I'm looking for him, something happens. I never know what it is, but I can't breathe. I try to drag in a breath but nothing comes through the snorkel, like something became lodged in the tube. That's when I wake up. I'm sure there's some psychological explanation for my mind conjuring that nightmare. If only I knew what it meant!

I sat up and swung my legs over the bedside, tiptoeing across the area rug into Freya's room. When I leaned against the side of her crib, my fingers carefully touched one of the dark curls on top of her head. She'd turned one last month and had become such a little stinker. My dad claimed she was just like me at that age. My mother had always complained about what I put her through, though I honestly haven't found Freya as challenging as my mother always claimed I was.

She really behaved no different than any curious and loving toddler. She liked to touch and explore and stayed constantly busy. My father, Jena, and Charlie all adored her, and I never lacked for someone to watch her when I needed it—not that those occasions happened often. The girls and I sometimes had a night out, but those were usually more dinner and a glass of wine rather than our older outings to the local bar or club. We'd become rather dull with Freya's birth.

Freya took a deep breath and sighed in her sleep, which made me smile. I didn't want to wake her, so I snuck back out and padded through to the kitchen to make coffee. Jena came in a moment later, grabbed her usual container of yogurt, and sat across the table from me while I had my required first dose of caffeine.

"I didn't get a chance to tell you last night," said Jena, breaking the silence, "but I made an appointment for a new client after you came upstairs yesterday. She's coming in with her father at two, and based on the wedding she described, I booked her in with you."

"Sounds good. Since I finished the Parker wedding this weekend, I have the time."

"We also need to decide if we're going to event plan for Christmas this year."

I swallowed my sip of coffee and nodded. When we first started, we were more of an all-around event planning company until we gained the reputation we needed and the steady clientele to stick with just weddings. Christmas, however, was always the exception. During those first few years, we gained several good corporate clients that paid well and were worth the extra work. Now that the business was solid and off the ground, we kept them more for the nice Christmas bonuses we received as a result. "We need to look at the weddings we have scheduled. I think we have one or two more than last year, which might make things difficult."

"Yes." Jena pointed with her spoon. "But you also aren't breastfeeding this year. Dad can always babysit, or even Micah. He loves playing with Freya."

I couldn't help but wince. Micah adored hanging out with Freya, but the few times he'd babysat her at night, he'd played with her instead of putting her to bed. Some nights, Freya played till she dropped, but then there were the nights she became wired—and those were the problem. Micah ended up going home around the time Freya became fussy and miserable. I could've beat him for doing that. I always spent the next hour walking and crooning her to sleep.

My hand flew up, palm out. "Not Micah. He's great for a playdate but not for babysitting. You know that."

"I know, but he's so desperate to adopt a child and his boyfriend isn't ready. He lives for the time he can spend with Freya."

"But he doesn't have to clean up the mess when he lets her stay up all night." Micah was such a sweetheart. While we were in college, he always called himself my gay boyfriend and was the perfect stand-in when I received unwanted attention from men in clubs. Plus, he was so much fun to go dancing with. He knew all the best places. I never went without a dance partner when he was around.

The security alarm beeped and Jena tilted back for a glimpse at the clock. "Maggie is here. I suppose I should get dressed. This morning, I'm taking the Grahams to Blooms to finalize the flowers."

"Good. They should've done that a month ago."

"I know." She stood and headed toward the kitchen. "I had to tell them they'd have to arrange the flowers themselves if they didn't make a decision soon. I also said I couldn't guarantee them live flowers, and they'd have to use fake. That got the mother in a tizzy."

That woman was as fake as they came and *so* into appearances. I could see her getting all worked up. Of course, she had no idea that artificial flowers didn't have to look cheap. We'd had a few clients use silk arrangements that were beautiful. "Nice thinking."

I stood and put my coffee cup in the dishwasher. "I need to take a shower, but I'll be down as soon as Freya is up. She shouldn't sleep much longer."

"No problem. I'll see you down there."

The shower was heavenly and helped continue what the coffee hadn't as far as waking me up. By the time I was dressed, Freya was sitting up in her crib talking gibberish to the crocheted raccoon Jena gave her for her birthday. She loved that thing. She wouldn't go anywhere without it, so we never left it behind.

"Good morning, sweet pea," I said softly when I entered the room. Freya smiled and stood, hugging her toy to her side while she bounced for me to pick her up. I kissed her little temple as I hoisted her to my hip. "Let's get you dressed. Then, we'll get you breakfast and go downstairs to work. What do you say?"

One nice thing about owning or co-owning your own company was that we made our own rules. Freya had toys in every office and even a play yard downstairs just in case we needed to keep her more contained. Really and truly, she was a pretty good baby. She played, and between the three of us and our new assistant Maggie, we kept her fairly occupied most of the day.

I changed her then fed her some yogurt and gave her a little sliced banana on her tray. Once she'd eaten that, I buttered a piece of toast and let her eat that on her own while I ate a quick bite. The door to the balcony opened and shut and the alarm beeped, however, it didn't bother me. Charlie had a key so she didn't have to walk around to the front in the mornings.

"There's the little stinker," she said when she came around the corner. Freya giggled and swung her legs, knocking her high chair. A huge grin lit Charlie's face. "If you want, I'll finish up and get her dressed while you go down. Aunt Charlie could use some Fay time this morning." She picked Freya up. "Yes, she could."

Thank goodness Charlie no longer whirled Freya around when she took her out of the seat! Charlie learned not to do that quickly. She did like to call her "Fay," but so far, no one else did. Most people used Freya.

I kissed my daughter's little head and gave her a quick scan before I left her with Charlie. I suppose it's a very mom thing to do but just to be sure nothing was wrong before I left. Freya smiled and made a smacking kissy noise, her little blue eyes twinkling with mischief. They'd never changed color. They still looked just like her dad's.

A list of things to do awaited me downstairs, so I thanked Charlie and headed down. After a phone call to a client, an email to another, and a call to one of the caterers in town, Charlie brought Freya in all dressed for the day and set her on a blanket in the corner.

"Okay, I've got bookkeeping to do. Let me know if you two need me."

"Thanks," I said as Charlie waved and strode out the door.

That day, I spent the morning making phone calls and played with my daughter. Fortunately, I was good at multi-tasking and kept a notepad handy in case I needed to write something down. She fell asleep easily for her afternoon nap, so I took the monitor downstairs to my office while I waited for the new client Jena told me about that morning.

At two o'clock sharp, Maggie peeked her head in. "Ellie, Miss Davies is here."

My stomach twisted into a heavy knot. "Did you say Davies?" I whispered as I stood and came around my desk.

Maggie's eyebrows drew down in the middle, and she stepped inside. "Yes, didn't Jena tell you?"

My head shook adamantly. "No, she only said I had a new client. Right before she left, she told me the time for the appointment. I didn't think to get a name." I peered through the door, but the old formal living room, now waiting room, was at a bad angle to be able to see through to get a glimpse of the client. "What's her first name? Do you know?"

"Addy. Why?"

I was going to vomit. It couldn't be the same Addy Davies, could it? Davies was a common enough name and so was Addy these days.

"Are you okay?"

"Yes, I'm sorry. You caught me by surprise is all."

Maggie didn't look convinced, but I smoothed the skirt of my dark blue sundress and swallowed hard, trying to calm my suddenly twisting and churning stomach while I walked to the door of the waiting area. A young woman sat in a chair in the corner reading one of our bridal magazines while an older man stared out the window. She could certainly be in her early twenties like William's sister. She looked like the photograph on his phone too.

"Hello," I said. I couldn't just stand there and gawk at them like an idiot. "My name is Ellie Barrett." Stepping forward, I held out my hand. Better to bite the bullet than give a bad impression!

"Oh." The young lady, who could only be Addy, stood and took my hand. "I'm Addy Davies." Her coloring and hair were just like William's—except the eyes. Hers were brown. "She held out her arm in the direction of the older man. "And this is my father, Grant."

My knees nearly gave out when I turned and my eyes met ones identical to my daughter's. "It's a pleasure." I have no idea how I managed to get that out without stuttering or sounding completely freaked out.

Mr. Davies smiled and nodded. "We've heard some wonderful things about your weddings and with my daughter still finishing up at the Boston Conservatory, we needed someone closer to arrange matters."

"You must be quite a musician." I clasped my hands in front of me to keep them from shaking.

"I don't know about that," she said while her cheeks pinked. "I think I just love to play my violin and would do it all day long if I could."

I liked that she didn't want to accept the compliment. She seemed down to earth. "I'm sure that's part of it, but you'd have to have talent as well."

"She does," said her father. "In spades."

I wrenched one of my hands-free and held it out toward my office. "If you'll join me, we'll discuss how to make your dream wedding a reality."

The smile that adorned Miss Davies' face was so genuine and happy. As frightened as I was of this, I didn't want to disappoint her. Besides, I would look absolutely certifiable if I suddenly refused to arrange her wedding. She wouldn't have had an appointment if we didn't have an opening for a client. Thank God, I'd cleaned! I'd thrown Freya's blanket in the wash and put her toys away in the cabinet.

"Will your fiancé be joining you?"

Her eyebrows drew down and she frowned. "He had to travel to New York for a performance. I hope that's not a problem."

"Please have a seat." I gestured to the chairs in front of my desk. "Of course not, but I didn't want to cover anything he might want a say in."

She glanced at her father and back. "He told me I could do whatever I wanted. I just need to tell him where to be, when to be there, and what to wear."

I laughed. "A very accommodating groom, then. Before we get started, would you care for some coffee, tea, champagne?"

"I don't need anything," she said.

Her father held up his hand. "I'm fine, thank you. Before we go too far, your associate said the distance wouldn't be an issue, but I want to make sure. I live in Savannah. We're having the wedding here because Addy's fiancé is from this area."

"It's not an issue at all. I assure you. If you're going to be in the Charleston area for a time, it would be best to arrange for some things now, such as the food and the cake. For example, most of the caterers we use will prepare a tasting so you can be sure of your choice."

"I'll only be in town for the weekend," said Addy. "I have to be back in Boston on Monday. If you can arrange those for a day or two, particularly around a holiday, I could fly back for it. I don't mind."

Her father raised his eyebrows. "Your brother and I could handle a few things. It's only a few hours."

My teeth clenched together in an effort not to make a face or gasp. Did Jena realize who she was booking? I couldn't imagine her doing this on purpose, but she'd always thought I should've told William about Freya. What if she recognized the name?

Miss Davies looked at me with a shrug. "If all else fails, we could do that. I'm afraid my tastes are different from my future mother-in-law. I'd prefer not to ask her if possible."

I plastered a smile on my face. "It's not a problem at all."

For two hours, I spoke with Miss Davies and her father about what she wanted, her timeline, and plans. When they left, I had a list of things to accomplish for Monday and I'd given her a list of bridal shops in the area so she could take a look around before she returned to school. If it was a necessity, she could always purchase a gown in Boston and ship it to us once it was altered so she wouldn't be packing it or carrying it on a plane.

After Addy and her father left, I avoided Jena until I put Freya to bed that evening. Once I was certain my daughter was out for the night, I knocked on my sister's bedroom door. When I entered, I shut the door behind me and leaned against it. "Why didn't you tell me the name of the clients today?"

Jena sat on her bed with her back against the headboard and a book propped on her legs. "I didn't make the appointment. Maggie simply told me yesterday that we had a new client. She'd said she'd booked them with you because you had the opening and because the initial questions the client answered indicated she would prefer your style over mine. What's the big deal?"

"Because her name is Addy Davies."

Her legs dropped flat onto the bed. "You've got to be shitting me."

If it'd been any other time and conversation, I would've laughed at Jena's uncharacteristic swear. "I wish I was. And guess what? She and her father might send William to do the tasting at the caterers and the bakeries."

"I'm sorry, but Maggie had no way of knowing."

"I know she didn't. I just can't believe the bad luck that they would walk into our offices."

"How did they hear about us? They aren't even from here, are they?"

I crossed one arm over my chest and chewed on the nail of my other hand. "No, Savannah. The groom is from this area, and they heard about us from somewhere. I didn't ask, but Maggie probably has it in their online questionnaire."

"Do you need me to take the account?"

"How bad would it look if I pass them off to you? We work as a team, but we can't just swap out the primary. I mean we've never done that before. I think it would look bad, don't you?"

"If you clicked with her, then yes, I think it would."

I started chewing on my lip. It was definitely a nervous habit, but I couldn't exactly scream out my frustration at the top of my lungs.

"What are you going to do?"

I sighed and shook my head. "Keep Freya out of the office if they're coming in for an appointment and hope they don't find out about her." They hadn't noticed her picture on my desk, but it didn't face toward them. I'd have to remember to move it the next time they came into the office.

"Ellie?"

I started, dropping my hand since I'd started biting my nail. "Hmm?"

"I said what if William isn't as bad as this man led you to believe?"

"I don't know. I might only see him at the wedding. I can stay busy enough to avoid him."

Jena shifted so she was sitting cross-legged. "When William discovers his little sister's wedding planner is the woman he fell in love with almost two years ago, I'd be willing to bet more money than I possess that he *will* show up before the wedding. You can't avoid this."

"Maybe she won't tell him." It was a long shot, but it was possible. Geez! I didn't even sound like I believed it!

"He's sent you mail here. He knows where you work. His sister or his father will at some point tell him who's organizing the wedding. When he finds out, he will come. If you're going to pretend otherwise, then you're lying to yourself, sweetheart."

She was right. I was screwed.

Chapter 13

I went about business as usual, concentrating on Freya and work. However, I was still shaken by Addy's sudden appearance and what that could mean. Would William come, or wouldn't he? After spending several days tied in knots, I gave myself a mental slap. I'd simply have to deal with whatever happened when it happened. Otherwise, I'd make myself sick worrying over all of the possibilities, and go crazy after a week or two. I didn't have any other choice. That's not true. I did have a choice. I could contact William now and get it over with. But how would that help?

The weekend after Miss Davies became a client, we had two weddings in the area—one in Charleston and one in a small town north of Marysville. After a wedding, either we'd immediately have a new client or we'd have a slight lull between the wedding and the next flurry of business. During a busy month like June, all three of us covered multiple weddings every weekend, but for September, two events every weekend created a bit more of an ease to our routines.

The following week, we continued on as always. We had appointments with existing clients, but mostly, we worked on those particular accounts, taking care of any loose ends and making sure we were up-to-date with the timelines.

Nothing was different or out of the ordinary, until Thursday, just after lunch, when Maggie appeared in my office. At the time, I had a bakery in Charleston on the phone, discussing quotes on a wedding cake, when she very nearly shimmied into the office, eyes wide, and pointing to the waiting area.

I held up a finger, but she started bouncing, which made me stare. What the heck was going on? Did we have a celebrity in the office? Maggie had never been an excitable employee though today's behavior made me reconsider.

"Yes, thank you. I'll expect those numbers by Monday. Of course. Thanks again." I hung up and looked at her. "What's going on?"

As I stood, she did that strange walk to my side and leaned toward my ear. "Hot guy. A seriously hot guy came in and asked for you specifically."

Suddenly, my knees wobbled as though they might buckle. I put a hand on my desk. Shit! It had to be him. Maggie knew most of the grooms as well as the locals so it couldn't be anyone else. "Did he give a name?"

"William Davies. You had an appointment with his sister, Addy. Remember?" She watched me for a moment and stepped a little closer. "Ellie? Honey, you're suddenly white as a sheet." She put her hands on my upper arms and caught my eye. "Are you sure you're okay? Do you want me to tell him that you're tied up for the rest of the day?" She sounded more like a southern grandmother than the twenty-nine-year-old that she was.

As much as I wanted to scream, *Yes! And get him out of the building!* I couldn't. I'd let the coward in me win out long enough. I had to face him at some point, and it might as well be today. We couldn't just happen to meet at his sister's wedding. That would be a disaster, not to mention extremely unprofessional of me. "No, I'll take care of it, thank you." I handed her Freya's baby monitor. "Would you give this to Jena or Charlie, please? I'll be in the park."

With a quick bob of the head, she took the device and hurried off while I pressed my palm to my stomach. "Here goes nothing," I whispered. With a deep breath in and back out, I began moving toward the front of the house.

A door opened, and I turned. Jena and Charlie poked their heads through and both gave me a thumbs up. Easy for them to say! They weren't the ones who had to talk to him. I didn't see how this was going to go well. I'd considered calling him on a number of occasions over the last year, usually when looking at Freya made me miss him so much my heart ached. The problem was that no matter how much I rehearsed it in my head, I didn't know how to tell him about his daughter without things going badly. What if he decided to take her from me? I wouldn't survive that.

I pulled my shoulders back a little and stood as tall as possible. I could do this. I *could* do this! Before I had the opportunity to second guess myself, I stepped around the door frame and William shot from his chair like a scalding hot poker touched his backside.

"Hello, William." I wish I could've come up with something creative or different—something like out of a novel, but my brain wouldn't cooperate. I rarely thought of something witty or clever in the moment. It didn't help that I trembled like I was bare-assed naked in the snow.

"Hi," he said, stepping closer. "I hope it's okay that I came here. I wanted to talk to you, if you don't mind."

Nodding, I motioned toward the door. "If you'd like, we can take a walk. There's a nice park across the street." I didn't want to wake up the baby if we started yelling. I also didn't want her to clue him in to her existence before I had the chance to tell him.

"That sounds good." He shoved his hands in his pockets but then pulled one out to rake his fingers through his hair. "Thank you."

I led the way through the door and down the steps, but it wasn't until we crossed the road that one of us spoke.

"You don't need to let them know where you're going?" he asked, giving a sort of turn back and pointing with his thumb toward the house.

"Maggie already knows."

God, I was going to be sick! I was scared shitless. It wasn't like I didn't have warning. Something in the pit of my stomach knew he'd come. Jena and Charlie kept saying he would come. My mind simply hadn't caught up. I still couldn't believe he stood beside me.

I took the turn that led to the pond. "I . . ." The words stuck in my throat. What was I supposed to say? I mean *Hi, William. I gave birth to your child* wasn't right. Jena would tell me to say it but this wasn't as easy as she would like to believe. He was here—walking next to me—and I'd put this off for so long—too long.

"I wanted to thank you." He cleared his throat but continued to walk with his hands in his pockets. "You could've turned Addy away last week, but you didn't, even though you had to know who she was. She heard your company's name from her future sister-in-law. I didn't even know she came until Monday when my father told me. He was unaware of who you were during the meeting, but once I told him, he had nothing but praise for how you treated Addy and listened so intently to her wishes."

"Your sister is lovely. Why wouldn't I want to help her?"

He stopped and faced me. "Because you would have to see me at the wedding. Because I should've been honest with you on the island and told you everything. Because I screwed up. I know I did, and I'm so sorry I hurt you. I don't blame you for not wanting to see me again."

I shook my head. I had a difficult time holding his gaze. "There are a number of reasons I didn't call you. I wanted to so badly at times, but you were still married. You might be separated and working on a divorce, but I had no way of knowing that until you contacted me. Once I knew you'd split with your wife, I didn't know how long it would take for you to be free of her. You even said she was contesting it. Then, there was this guy—"

His body jerked as he straightened. "A guy?"

"It's not what you're thinking." I put both hands out in front of me, palms toward him. "When I received your package, I walked to that bench over there." I pointed to where I always sat when I came to the park to think. "After I read your letter, I cried. That's when a man approached to ask if I was okay. He saw the return address on the envelope and claimed he knew you—that he'd worked for Davies Construction."

"He did?" His voice held an odd note I didn't recognize.

"He said your father hired him and how he'd been saving money for school, but you fired him for no reason other than you didn't like him. He claimed your wife was this paragon, how she volunteered for charity and went to church every Sunday on her own."

His chuckle came out sarcastic and harsh. I flinched. "Claire? Volunteer? The closest she gets to charity is dropping off last season's wardrobe at Goodwill, and I've never known her to attend church. You believed him?"

"I didn't know what to believe."

"You didn't know him! You do know me!" The low voice I loved had disappeared for a bit higher, louder version.

I glanced around. Luckily, no one was in this part of the park, but I still wanted to calm him if I could. "I'd known you for what—nine or ten days? You'd left out the fact that you were married. I had to answer your wife's phone call to discover what you should've told me from the beginning. I was so confused, I didn't know what to do. It terrified me that you might not be the man I fell in love with. What if I trusted you again, and it bit me on the ass? I wouldn't have survived it, William. I couldn't do it."

"But you trusted a complete stranger. I have no idea who in the hell he was, but I can tell you that if I fired him, I had documented proof it was required. I have workers I don't care for on my crews, but as long as they do their job, I have no problem with them. I'm not their friend. I'm their boss."

I'd turned to look at him while he defended himself. At some point, he'd removed his hands from his pockets, and now, emphasized points that he made with his index finger. "It was a difficult time." It was a lame excuse.

He raked his hands through his hair. "If you'd called and talked to me, I could've proven myself to you. I tried to call and you refused to speak with me, so I gave you some time and worked on getting my life in order. And instead of giving me a chance, you let a total stranger come between us?"

"There wasn't an us at the time." I almost whispered the words. I remembered why I'd avoided this. It hurt like hell. Even after almost two years, seeing his face was still just as painful. My eyes burned, and I had a lump the size of a baseball in my throat.

"Because you wouldn't take a chance!" he said. "That day, you didn't even let me know you were going. You left without a word."

I shook my head and crossed my arms over my chest. "You have no idea! I had to get away. I had to be able to think. I couldn't do that with you there. I couldn't take the chance that you'd talk me into continuing what we'd started!" My eyes burned, so I squeezed them tight and reopened them. "I took the next plane out, but I could only go as far as London. I spent the next three days in art museums trying to forget about you and how miserable I was. It was how I coped."

He shoved his hands back in his pockets. "It didn't take much to figure out what you'd done. I saw housekeeping go inside not long after you left. I followed you to the airport, you know. You'd mentioned having a stopover in Rome and how you'd wished it was longer so you could go into the city for the day. Your plane left the island just before I got there." He looked out over the water. "I packed my luggage and managed to get on a flight later that evening." His layover had been in Dubai both ways from what I remembered.

"I had no reason to stay with you gone," he said. "I landed in Atlanta, drove straight to my dad's house, and filed for divorce as soon as my lawyer could draw up the paperwork. I lived with my father until Claire's attorneys advised her she needed to give up. I had a post-nuptial agreement and photos of her kissing and touching another man. I still can't believe dissolving that farce of a marriage took a year. I almost called you the day I received the final documents, but I'd convinced myself you still didn't want to talk to me."

"You can't blame me for being scared." My voice came out hoarse, almost a whisper. "Anyone hurt in that way would be gun shy."

"Gun shy? You don't even know that man's name and you trusted him over me." He clenched and released his jaw. "How can you ever explain that?"

I wiped a tear from my cheek. "I've told you why. We hardly knew one another."

His finger pointed at my chest. "That's not true! I told you more about myself than anyone! I opened myself up to you completely!"

"Except you didn't tell me about your wife!"

"Ex-wife and unofficially had been for a while!"

I threw my hands up and dropped them to my sides. "Just because your marriage had been over as far as you were concerned doesn't excuse not telling me. You were still married!"

"I was wrong and I've admitted that," he said more calmly. "If the situation were reversed, I wouldn't have listened to someone I'd never met before over you. I would've trusted you over anyone."

"You have no way of knowing what you would or wouldn't do! That's unfair and you know it! I told you it was a difficult time! I had so much going on, I wasn't sleeping well, and I couldn't think straight! I didn't know what to do!"

William pivoted to face me, leaning closer as he said, "Do you think you were the only one? Do you think I didn't have nights where I would lie awake wondering what you were doing? I had so many times where I wanted to jump in the car and drive here to see you. It took everything I had to respect your wishes and concentrate on work!"

My body shook and I squeezed my eyes shut. "It's not the same!" I couldn't take this for long. The yelling was just too much.

"Like hell, it isn't!"

"It couldn't be because you weren't the one who was moody, hormonal, and pregnant!"

Chapter 14

"What did you say?" He staggered back a step, his face ashen.

"I didn't mean to tell you that way. I'm sorry, I'm so sorry." The words came out softly and I wrapped my arms around my middle, my stomach squeezing in on itself more and more the longer he stared agape and nothing emerged from his mouth. As the seconds ticked by, he stood silent while my heart rose further and further into my throat. Lord, my eyes burned, making me blink back tears. "Please say something."

"You were pregnant?" His disbelief echoed through every word, making my insides twist more than they'd been before.

"Yes." I nodded as though he needed the emphasis. I don't know why. He was an intelligent man. He didn't require it.

"But we never forgot protection. I don't understand." He concentrated on the ground with his forehead creased. My arms rose slightly with an overwhelming urge to hold him, but the gesture wouldn't be appreciated. His stiff posture made it obvious.

"We did, but if you remember, a couple of condoms broke while we tried to put them on. Maybe there was something wrong with one of them, and we didn't realize it. I don't know. When I came home, I couldn't get rid of this nausea. I thought it was stress and the fact that I was heartbroken. At first, it probably was, but I started to feel worse, my period never came, and at times, I couldn't hold down food at all. That was when Jena made me take a home pregnancy test."

He wouldn't look at me, and it made me jumpy. His head remained down, and he'd started kicking at the pathway—hard.

He was going to explode at some point, but when? Considering the bombshell I'd just laid on him, he was entirely too calm.

All of a sudden, his head lifted and his glare bored so deeply into me I should've had a hole gouged into my skull. "How long after the island did you know?"

"About two or three weeks." My voice was weak and shaky.

"And you never tried to tell me? In all this time, you couldn't be bothered to pick up a phone and let me know I have a child?"

His eyes never left mine. I couldn't look away. "I've picked up the phone so many times . . ."

"But you never actually dialed. You never actually made the call."

I shook my head and swallowed. "No. I was terrified at first, and the longer I waited, the harder it became."

He raked his fingers through his hair again, but this time, he tugged on his neck before he flung his hands back down to his sides. "But you'll tell me now. Why is that so easy all of a sudden? Did you abort it? Are you telling me this to hurt me?"

My eyes had closed when he began speaking again, but at his accusation, they flew open. "God, no! I couldn't. I don't know how you could even think that."

"Well, since it seems you were correct—we didn't know one another as well as we thought. Because if you'd asked me before today whether you'd keep something like this from me, I would've said, 'No way.' I would've been willing to bet everything I owned that you would tell me if something so important happened. I was wrong though, wasn't I? You didn't breathe a word, so I have every reason to ask you that question. Don't I?"

The tears I'd tenuously been holding at bay couldn't be held back anymore and began to track down my cheeks. "I'm so sorry."

"You're sorry! That's great. You're sorry." He laughed, but with this high-pitched edge that made me flinch and stiffen. "I suppose I should be thrilled you're telling me now? I have a child somewhere. I don't know if it's a boy or a girl. I don't know a name or what it looks like. I don't even know how fucking old it is at this point."

My arms wrapped tighter around my middle. "You have a daughter. She was six pounds when she was born so she was a little thing. She has your eyes and her hair color is darker, like yours."

He cleared his throat and began blinking rapidly. "Stop. Please. Just for a minute. I can't . . ." He walked over to the closest bench, sat down, propped his elbows on his knees, and put his head in his hands. "Why did you bring me out here?" His voice was so quiet, I almost missed the question.

"Because if we talked the way we needed to, I thought we might argue. It would be unprofessional to do that in the office. I also live upstairs, so any argument could still be heard by everyone, and Freya was taking her nap."

"Freya?" His head shot up and his eyes stared at me without blinking. "You named her after my mother?"

"Yes, I named her Freya Elizabeth. I didn't know your mother's middle name so I chose a different one. I'd show you a picture, but I didn't bring my phone. She should be awake in another half-hour. If you want to meet her, that is."

His head dropped back down to face the ground, and a shuddering breath wracked his body. "Did you think I'd be such a terrible father?" The tremor in his voice made it pretty obvious he was crying, and my heart tore in two. I'd hurt him horribly. Would he ever understand or forgive me?

"I was terrified, William. I didn't know what to do, and I'd only known you a short time. That man I met in the park didn't help. He painted a pretty bad image of you. Mostly, I was afraid of getting my heart shattered again."

It was my fault. As badly as he hurt me, I turned around and did something equally atrocious if not worse to him. At the time, it seemed necessary, but now, I wanted more than anything to go back and do it all over again. If he'd really been the person that guy described, he would've behaved differently when I blurted out that he was a father. He wouldn't be in such pain. He was too wounded, too emotional to be so callous toward others.

I swallowed the lump in my throat. "If you want, we could head back. I do think we need to talk more, but you might be more comfortable upstairs, and then, when Freya wakes up, you could see her."

Without a word, he wiped his face with his hands and stood. I started walking and he fell into step beside me, his hands in tight fists at his sides. Was I doing the right thing? He was angry. But how angry? Would it be something he could get past so we could work together to raise our daughter? Would I lose my daughter because I finally bit the bullet and told him?

We crossed the street, and he stopped on the sidewalk and surveyed the house. "You were searching for a new office two years ago. Was this where you moved?"

"Yes, Jena found it just before I learned I was pregnant and suggested it after the home pregnancy test came back positive. We hadn't been considering an investment like this; however, the three of us combined paid more in rent than the mortgage on this house. Because we all live here, I've rarely needed help with Freya. The few times I have, my dad or a friend usually babysits." He didn't nod or smile. I didn't know what to do to make things better, but oh, how I wanted to!

I led the way up the steps and inside. Maggie lifted her eyebrows as the door closed behind me. She must have thought we were both a mess. We'd both been crying, and no doubt, it showed, but she didn't say a word. When we headed toward my office, the door to Jena's flew open and Micah stepped out.

"I told you someone came in," he said loudly, waving his hand then dropping it so it hung limply from his wrist. "There you are, sweetheart." He drawled the words as he stepped up and kissed both of my cheeks in that European style he always favored. "Jena and Charlie insisted I come back tomorrow, but why would I do that when you're here now." He reached into his man's bag. I called it a purse, but he refused to be quite that feminine—funny for a man who wore more eyeliner than I did. "The pictures of Freya arrived, and I wanted to run them over. I'm still excited at how well they came out, but then that daughter of yours is very photogenic. She must get it from her father." He chuckled at his own joke and rolled his eyes when neither Jena nor Charlie joined him.

He shoved a large envelope into my hand and glanced around the room. "Where is that little cherub of yours anyway and when do I get to spend some more daddy time with her?"

I closed my eyes and my teeth clenched. Jena gasped and Charlie muttered something under her breath that I couldn't make out. I probably didn't want to know, knowing Charlie as well as I did.

Micah had no idea what was going on. I had to remember that or I'd kill him with my bare hands. As I turned toward my office, William just stood there, his jaw pulsing near his ear. His eyes drilled into Micah, who grinned widely and winked. "Well, hello," he drawled.

My hands lifted palm out to William. "It's not what you think." Not that I knew what he really thought. But he needed to know that Micah had in no way ever acted as a daddy stand-in for William. I have no idea if he heard me or not because as I started speaking, he gave me a fleeting glance, strode past, and out the front door, slamming it behind him.

As I ran after him, Charlie slapped Micah on the back of the head. "Fuck, Micah. One of these days you need to invest in a damn filter for that mouth of yours."

William was already in the car, starting it while I struggled to run down the steps in my heels. Today, I cursed my penchant for pretty dresses and shoes. They hampered my ability to catch him. He pulled away from the curb and drove away before I could do anything about it.

I threw up my arms and waved them back and forth. "William!" They dropped to my sides and I turned to the house. That was when I heard the tell-tale sound of Freya crying. Every last muscle in my body slumped.

"Micah arrived just before you returned." When I looked up, Jena stood in the front porch. "Charlie and I shoved him into my office and tried to keep him quiet, but you came back before we could explain things to him. I'm sorry."

"It's not your fault. It's mine for waiting so long to tell William the truth."

She hugged me when I made it back up the steps. "Are you okay?"

"I don't know. I was so afraid to trust William, then I wanted to but I'd waited so long. I was ashamed to have kept it from him. I figured this would all blow up in my face. I've been a hideous coward."

"At least you finally did it. He knows. We just have to pray he comes around."

I drew back and shrugged, trying to hold in my tears. "I've hurt him dreadfully. After the way he behaved when he learned about Freya, I know he'll come back to be her father, but I don't know if he'll want me too. I'm not sure I blame him either."

"You've both hurt one another," said Jena in that motherly way she had. "If you can both forgive, then maybe you'll have a chance."

"Look! There's Mommy." Charlie placed Freya on the floor, and she ran over to me with her hands up.

I stepped inside, swept my daughter into my arms, and kissed her cheek. "We have nothing to do but wait and see now."

Micah came out of Jena's office. "I swear. Y'all should've told me Ellie's baby daddy was here. I wouldn't have said that if I'd known." He kissed my cheeks again. "*Pardonnez-moi* if I made a mess of things." He followed by also kissing Jena's and Charlie's cheeks. "I only stopped by to give you the photos. I have to run. I'm taking some engagement photos at sunset. I have to get prepped or it will be a total wreck. Tata!" He gave a girly wave and hurried out.

"That man is a walking hurricane," said Charlie. "He whirls in with a lot of noise and wind and never fails to leave destruction in his wake."

"Stop it," I said, chiding. "He has a good heart."

Charlie sighed. "He still fu—screwed things up." Charlie rubbed my daughter's back as I held her, her little cheek resting near my shoulder. "Why don't we grill and drink tonight? Fajitas and Margaritas?"

"How about just steak and red wine?" I didn't want complicated. Today had been complicated enough. "I need to get out for a bit. I'll get Freya a snack, and I'll go to the store. Anyone need anything else while I'm there?"

"We'll text you if we think of anything," said Jena.

I peered down at my dress. I didn't want to stay in work clothes, so I went upstairs and set Freya on the floor of my room with a plate of puffy toddler snacks. I threw my blue pumps into my closet and took off my sundress, throwing it in the hamper before I took out a pair of denim shorts and a black sleeveless top. We were grilling, so I pulled my hair into a fishtail and secured it so it hung over my shoulder. I didn't want it in the way later.

Freya babbled to her raccoon while I strapped her into her stroller and continued on while I walked her through the park. The grocery store wasn't too far and my baby girl had always loved going for a walk. When I entered the store, the air conditioning hit me like an icy wave, so I pulled to the side of the door and put Freya's sweater on her.

I picked up a few vegetables we could put on the grill. The less we had to clean in the kitchen the better as far as I was concerned. I made a pass through the meat department then grabbed a few items for Jena and Charlie and some baby food for Freya. As I turned onto the aisle with the wine, my eyes met some very familiar ones in front of me.

"Miss Barrett," he said.

"Mr. Davies, I didn't know you were in town? And call me Ellie . . . please."

"As you know by now, my son came to see you. I admit to using the excuse of a nearby building project as a reason to tag along."

I tried to smile but it likely turned out flat. "I'm sure he appreciates your company."

He did manage to get a slight curve to his lips. "I hope he does." He knelt down and gave a full, genuine smile to Freya, touching her little nose with his finger. "You're beautiful, sweetheart. You look so much like your father and Addy when they were your age. Of course, Addy's eyes are a different color."

"I think she looks more like William every day."

Glancing up at me, he nodded. "They were both good babies. My wife and I never had reason to complain."

"Freya has always been easy—easy to take care of, easy to love. She's never been demanding or fussy."

He stood and gaped. "Freya?"

"Yes. Didn't William tell you?"

He looked back down at her. "No, he left out that part. Thank you. His mother would be over the moon."

"William loved her a lot." It sounded presumptuous from me, considering.

"They were quite close." He glanced back down at Freya.

I swallowed the nerves bouncing around in my gut, moved around the stroller, and unfastened my daughter. When I had her propped on my hip, I pointed to Mr. Davies. I guess better late than never. "Freya, this is your grandpa. Can you say hi?" She put her head on my shoulder and held her raccoon a little tighter.

He smiled. "She's just as shy as William was too."

"Let's take a walk, sweetie." I set her on the floor and took her hand. "But let's leave your toy in the stroller." We took a couple of steps and I peered over my shoulder. "She loves walking while she holds someone's hand. If you want, it would be the best way for her to get to know you."

He stepped up to Freya's other side and offered her his hand. When she took it, he chuckled. We walked up and back down the wine aisle. As we headed toward the stroller, I took a deep breath. "I know you have to be pretty angry at me, but I *am* sorry I hurt him." I picked my daughter up and held her to my side.

"I was upset for my son when he told me what happened, but I have a little more clarity than he does at the moment. Neither of you are innocent in this relationship, and neither committed a minor transgression. Only the two of you can decide what can be salvaged from that. Whether you move forward together or on your own, you have a child together. Anger and animosity won't help her, and it won't help the two of you."

He was right. I hadn't been angry at William for a long time, but he would require time to get over his anger at what I'd done.

"He needs to think and cool off. I'd be willing to wager that you'll see him at some point in the next few days."

I put Freya back in her stroller and grabbed my purse. "I don't want to put you in the middle and I know I have no right to ask, but would you do something for me?"

He gave her a sidelong look. "That depends on what it is."

Most people didn't keep actual photos these days due to the accessibility of phones and photo apps not to mention social media, but I kept a small album of Freya's pictures with me. I hadn't added the new ones Micah'd dropped off an hour or two ago. Some of his others were in there, including my maternity photos. For some reason, Freya loved when I flipped through the pages so she could see them. I'd kept her occupied more often than I could count with that little book.

"Would you give him this?" I passed the album over. "It's not much, but I'd like for him to have it. The friend who came to the office today is the photographer who took the professional shots in there. I've known him forever, but he's only babysat Freya a handful of times and he behaved more like a bad uncle when he did."

"How's that?" Mr. Davies head tilted while he watched me.

"Micah doesn't put her to bed on time—he spoils her."

Mr. Davies' shoulders shook while he looked down at the leather cover on the book. "I understand."

I pointed to the shelves. "We're grilling tonight. I better grab the wine and get back before I start getting a million texts wondering where I am. I hope to see you again soon." After a strange and awkward arm motion toward the wine, I started to walk forward.

"Ellie?"

I stopped. "Thank you for introducing me to my granddaughter."

I nodded and smiled. "You're welcome."

Chapter 15

I spent the next day sporting a colossal case of the jitters that weren't from my coffee addiction. The steak and wine the night before were wonderful, but I'd picked at my food, hardly eating any of it. I hadn't even finished one glass of wine, and I hadn't slept well either. I dreamed William had returned angry, and the next thing I knew, Freya had disappeared. I searched everywhere for her, but I couldn't find her anywhere. I was frantic. Anytime I fell asleep, I had some variation of the same dream. I woke up with a start every time.

That morning, an enormous cup of coffee hadn't improved my dreadful mood. I snapped at Charlie and walked out of Jena's office when I disagreed with her. I just wasn't myself.

"Hey." When I looked up from the flower order in front of me, Charlie was leaning against the door frame with her arms crossed in front of her. "I know you're worried and that's why you're crabby, but Jena and I both agree you should take the rest of the day off. Take a nap with Fay then go to the park. It'll make you feel better."

"Okay," I said, sighing while I put my pen down. "I'm sorry. I didn't—"

"Jena heard you pacing most of the night. She knows you didn't sleep well. It's okay. We all have our crappy days. Your dad was only supposed to babysit until lunchtime so you need to go up to feed Fay anyway."

I didn't argue. There was no point because Charlie was right. If I was lucky, I might get two or three hours to sleep while Freya napped, but I'd stared at the order in front of me for the last hour. I wasn't getting anything done.

Charlie received a hug from me when I passed her on my way out of the door. "Thanks."

"Don't mention it. Y'all did practically the same for me when I broke up with Jensen, remember."

She'd broken up with him before college, but we'd definitely helped keep her sane. Instead of arguing, I nodded and trudged up the stairs, dad's voice becoming louder as I reached the top. I followed the sound into Freya's room where he was lying on the floor covered from head to toe in toys. Freya held another above him, poised to add to the pile when she saw me.

"Mama!"

I picked her up and kissed her cheek. "Are you burying Grandpa? Where did you get that idea?"

"I have no clue." Dad, chuckled, stood, and started tossing toys back in her basket. "She had a great time burying me one toy at a time, though."

"Are you hungry? We have leftover steak."

He straightened and leveled me with a look over his glasses. "Since when do you girls leave steak? I always have to guard mine with my life when I eat over here."

I rolled my eyes. We weren't that bad. "I wasn't very hungry last night. I'm going to warm it up and thought I'd ask if you wanted to share."

"No, thanks," he said. He had that look reserved for when he was trying to figure something out. "But why don't I sit with you. You can tell me what's going on."

I walked into the kitchen with Freya as Dad followed behind me. "Why do you think something's going on?"

"Because I know you, Ellie." He pulled out a seat and sat next to Freya's high chair while I fastened the safety straps. "You look exhausted."

"Thanks, Dad. I love you too."

"I heard you snap at someone from up here and that's nearly an entire ribeye you just pulled out of the fridge. The last time you ate that little, you were pregnant." His eyes popped.

"No! I'm not pregnant."

He held out his hands in front of him, palms facing me. "I know a woman can do it all on her own these days, but forgive me if I'm old fashioned and would prefer to have you married if you want another."

One side of my lips tugged upward. "*I'd* like to be married before I think about another." I sighed. "Yes, I'm upset about something, but I don't know what's going on. It's complicated."

"Very few things in life aren't complicated. Still, I might be able to help."

I put my steak in a skillet and turned it on. "I saw Freya's father yesterday."

He started and his eyes widened a little. "I thought he lived far away."

"Not *so* far." I gave a one-shouldered shrug and scratched at a fruit sticker stuck to the counter. "Savannah."

"Savannah," he said louder. "That's fairly close."

I took out what I needed for Freya's lunch and started to prep it. "If you remember, you asked me about him and I said he didn't live around here. I also told you I didn't want to talk about it."

"That's true. You were so stubborn."

I didn't know how to get around it, so I laid it all out—well, the filtered version of things, at least. When I was done, he gaped at me a moment then ran his hand across his mouth.

"Shit, Ellie." My father rarely swore. The fact that he had meant I'd really and truly shocked him. "Excuse me, but both of you have made mistakes. Tremendous mistakes. Thing is, you've had time to forgive him, but he hasn't had the same. I don't think he'll take too long since it's time away from his child. He's already missed a year of her life. Your idea to give his father the album was a good one. Let's hope it helps."

I handed Dad Freya's lunch but didn't let go until he looked me in the eye.

"What if he decides to take her away from me?"

He took my hand and squeezed. "I think it's doubtful. If this man's harbored feelings for you for two years, I don't believe he'll behave that way, but if he does, we'll get you a good lawyer and fight him. I'll pitch in on the cost if you need the money."

I kissed his forehead. "Thanks, Daddy." When I returned to making my lunch, I paused and leaned against the counter. "Can I ask you a question?"

He laughed and nodded. "You ask me questions all of the time. Shoot."

"Why did you stay with Mom for so long? I can't remember a time when the two of you got along. Why did you stay?"

After he blew out a long breath, he sat back and folded his arms over his chest. "To tell you the truth, it was because I didn't have a fancy prenup like your young man. When I divorced your mother, she took half of everything, just like I expected. It took me a long time before I was willing to part with that much.

"Seriously? You stayed because of money."

"I also had you girls to think of. I should've left a long time before I did, because as it turned out, you were better off without her. The problem was that I would've had to fight tooth and nail for custody of Jena. It was easier to leave things as they were."

I joined him at the table and picked at my food while he fed Freya. In the end, he finished my steak since I couldn't reheat it again. When he departed, I cleaned up Freya and changed clothes. When I was done, I caught myself staring into the backyard from the kitchen window. "Let's go outside. It's cooler today than yesterday but still nice enough that we can cuddle in the hammock. What do you think?"

She nestled her little face close to my neck, and I took that as an agreement, so I walked downstairs and through the original kitchen where Charlie sat at the table drinking tea and plugging away on her laptop.

"We're going to go lie in the hammock for a while."

Charlie glanced up and gave a thumbs up. "It's the perfect day for it. I've thought about going on the balcony and sitting in one of the wicker chairs while I work on figures."

I padded barefoot through the grass and across a few stepping stones to the hammock Dad had strung up between two trees. Because I liked to sit in the garden with Freya, he made sure it was a solid fabric one rather than rope so her little arms wouldn't get caught. On pretty days, it was one of my favorite places.

My daughter was almost asleep by the time I got comfortable. She lay on my stomach with her head on my chest while I caressed her soft curls with my fingertips. A cool breeze rattled the leaves on the trees around me as I let my eyes drift closed for just a second.

The tell-tale knock of a woodpecker foraging for food somewhere nearby rattled in my ear. Despite the occasional pauses, the tapping remained steady until my eyes gradually fluttered open. My arms were still wrapped around Freya, and other than her head having turned at some point, she still slept quietly on my front.

I'd breathed, stretched my legs, and shifted a little to get comfortable when something moved and drew my eye. Oh my God! It was William! He sat quietly along the edge of the patio, not far from where we were, his elbows on his knees, staring down at his clasped hands. When he peered up, his eyes met mine.

His eyes sported dark circles under them and his jaw was covered with a day of stubble. He looked tired—just as exhausted as I'd been a short time ago. How long had he been there? How long had I been asleep?

I held up my finger and carefully rolled so Freya lay on her side. The trick was always detangling myself without waking her. I snuck a quick peek at my watch, which read three o'clock. She'd be waking soon anyway, but if she slept for a bit longer, maybe William and I could talk.

It only took a minute or so before I was completely on my feet while my daughter still dozed quietly in the hammock. As

I turned, William stood a few paces away. "I wanted to thank you for this." He spoke in soft tones while he held out the album. "My father poured us each a glass of scotch last night and we talked—a lot. He relayed your message about your friend too."

"Good," I said just as quietly. "I hoped he would." He opened his mouth as though he might speak again, but I lightly touched his wrist. "We do need to talk. Why don't we pull a couple of chairs over? I think we'd both be more comfortable sitting, but I don't want to be too far away in case Freya wakes up. She could fall."

He glanced at our daughter and handed me the album so he could bring two chairs closer to the trees. When we both sat, I handed him back the book. "I'd like you to keep it. I have plenty of copies of these. I'd be happy to get you larger prints of some of them if you'd like."

His fingers hesitantly closed around the binding. "Thank you. I would love more if you have them. It was hard to look at them at first, but in the end, I stayed up most of the night poring over them. She's beautiful."

I couldn't help but laugh. "I'm sorry, but while I agree with you that she's beautiful, I find it funny. She resembles you so much more than me."

His lips barely turned up on the sides. "She has my eyes and hair color, but I don't know about the rest. Dad seems to think she has your smile." He gave me a mock scowl. "Are you saying I'm not beautiful?"

I smiled and shook my head. "I didn't say that. I usually use words more like handsome, devastatingly attractive." I finally got a real smile out of him and my insides somersaulted. "What is your father doing today?"

"Checking on a project an hour north of here. He'll be back this evening."

I rubbed one hand with the other while I looked at them. "I'm so sorry I didn't tell you about Freya. I'm also sorry you discovered the way you did. I never meant to blurt it out that way."

He sighed and leaned forward onto his knees as he'd been earlier. "Both of us made huge mistakes. I won't say that I'm not still hurt, but I hurt you terribly as well. As much as I wish you'd trusted me, you had no reason to believe me other than my word and that hadn't been too reliable."

I dropped back into my chair. "Jena tried to talk me into calling you—even Charlie tried to convince me in the labor room. They both worried I'd regret it later. I understand more of their perspective now. I'm glad we're not having this conversation ten or fifteen years into the future. You'd have lost nearly all of our daughter's childhood."

The hammock swayed and I jumped to make sure Freya didn't fall. With a heart-warming smile, she held up her arms and I lifted her to me. When I sat, I tried to get her to sit facing William, but she insisted on cuddling to my chest. She could see him, at least, so I pointed to him. "Freya," I whispered near her forehead. "Can you say 'hi' to your daddy?" She rubbed her face against my shoulder, but when she stopped, she watched him intently.

"Once she's awake, she'll be more willing to give you a chance."

"It's okay. As much as I'd love for her to come to me, I don't want to force her. It'd only make it take longer."

I peered back at the hammock. "I think her raccoon is still there. It's her favorite toy. Maybe if you hold it?"

He retrieved the little crocheted animal and put it on his knee, making Freya's head pop up. She frowned and turned to me.

"Why don't you go get it? He'll give it to you."

She shimmied down and stepped over to William as he leaned forward. She glanced back at me, but I waved her forward. "Go on."

Her hand timidly reached out for her stuffed animal and William handed it to her. "Hello," he said. "Do you like raccoons?" She held out the toy, and he smiled. "It's a very nice one. Did your aunt make that? I remember she once made your mommy some very nice things." She babbled off some nonsense and returned to me while he chuckled.

"Jena did make it for her. She knits and crochets while she watches movies and TV. Freya's always had a variety of hats and little sweaters to choose from. I don't know where to put them all when she outgrows them because I don't want to get rid of them." I quickly peeked back at the house. "I need to change her and get her a snack. Do you want to come inside and spend some more time with her? You can read her a book. She loves to be read to."

He nodded and stood as I did. "I would. I would love that. Thank you."

Chapter 16

When we went inside, we didn't run across Charlie or Jena on our way, which was a bit unusual. I had a feeling they were making themselves scarce, but I wouldn't know for sure until the end of the day.

William followed me into Freya's room, scanning the surroundings while I settled her on the changing table. "How much of her room did you decorate before she was born?" he asked.

I glanced around to the white tree that stretched up one corner and branched out onto the pale grey wall. "My dad painted and stenciled the tree branch. Freya was crazy stubborn whenever I had an ultrasound. Her feet were always in the way, so we couldn't tell she was a girl. I felt certain she was a girl, but just in case, I wanted a neutral theme I could build upon." I laughed. "Dad thought I was nuts to put down a white rug."

"So, you added the rest after she was born."

"Yes, Jena made the pink blankets and the pillow on the chair. I painted the raccoon watercolor a month or so ago after she made that toy her permanent companion." I put her bloomers back on and pointed to a basket of books. "If you'll pick one, the two of you can read while I get her snacks and some fruit ready."

I set her on the floor, and when she noticed what William was doing, she hurried over and pulled one out, holding it out to him.

"Do you want that one?"

"Sit on the floor," I mouthed when he looked up at me.

When he did, she turned and backed up to him, plopping down right on his lap. He opened the book and his deep voice started telling the tale while she watched the pictures and pointed to the different animals.

My eyes burned as tears gathered in my eyes. This was how it was supposed to be, but could I finally have everything I'd always wanted? Until this moment, I'd never let myself believe it was possible. I was so close. What would I do if it all fell apart now?

It didn't take long to have Freya's food ready, but before I could return for them, William walked in almost bent in half, holding Freya's hand. "I finished the book and she noticed you were gone. She took my hand to go looking for you."

"Well, y'all are just in time. If you'll put her in her chair, she can eat. I thought that if you want, we can go to the park after. She loves the swings. Then, we can make dinner." He fumbled a bit strapping her in but looked up at me while he held the tray.

I was assuming a lot about the rest of the day. Perhaps too much? "If you can't, then I understand. I thought—"

"No, I'd like to. I was supposed to leave tomorrow, but my father is going back to hold the office down so I can be here. I'd like to spend as much time with Freya as I can." He stood up straight. "How do I attach this?"

I smiled and showed him. My fingers touched his when I handed him the bowl of blueberries cut in half. I put some yogurt bites on her tray and she started to eat while we both watched like she was a show on stage.

I mentally shook myself to curb my nerves. "What would you like for dinner? When it doesn't rain, we usually grill. We can see what seafood the store has after we go to the park?"

"That sounds good." He took the seat by our daughter and picked up one of the yogurt bites for her to take from him.

I wanted him to bond with our daughter, so I tried to hide in the background. If I wasn't right there, she would keep interacting with him more than me. While the two of them became more comfortable with one another, I went and grabbed her sweater just in case it cooled off a few more degrees before we left for the park. I brought mine as well.

When Freya was finished, we headed downstairs to get the stroller out of the mud room off the old kitchen. She didn't seem to mind being held by William so I pulled the stroller from its storage spot and followed William toward the front door. Jena was in her office as we walked down the hall so I held up my hand.

She mouthed, "Park?"

I nodded and followed William outside. Once we crossed the street, I opened the stroller, but Freya pushed out her bottom lip and gave me the fiercest glare she could, grabbing his neck and holding on for dear life. He startled and laughed.

"It's okay, sweet pea," I said. "I won't make you get in. If you want Daddy to hold you, we'll just use your stroller for the shopping."

William headed through the gate, and Freya relaxed with one of her arms around his shoulders as I followed. I'd never seen Freya warm up to someone so fast, but maybe she understood more than I gave her credit for.

She had the best time while William pushed her in the toddler swing. He even stood in front of her and she'd giggle like crazy when she would swing in his direction. After, he held her while he controlled her sliding down a portion of the slide and helped her rock on one of those bouncy animals they had for toddlers. I even laughed at the sight of him on that toy, sort of awkwardly sitting behind her.

"Where's your phone?" I said, holding out my hand. "You have to have a picture of the two of you like that."

He pressed the screen to unlock it and handed it to me with the camera on. I backed up a few steps and snapped a photo while he leaned forward so his face was beside hers.

"If you want, I can take a picture of the three of you."

I jumped and swung my head around to find Charlie's brother Brandon standing behind me. "It's okay . . ."

"Elle, come on." William gestured me over, so I handed Brandon the phone and stepped beside them. I put a hand by Freya's on the handle and leaned over her opposite shoulder.

"Say cheese!" said Brandon.

I smiled as much as I could, but my entire body knew William was close—so very close, and he'd called me "Elle." Did he do it intentionally, was it a habit from memories, or was it the name he'd called me ever since the island?

"Thank you," I said to Brandon as I claimed William's phone. "How are you?"

"I'm good. Tell Charlie that Mom expects her for Sunday dinner this week and not to forget. You and Jena are invited, too, if you want, but you know that." He looked over my shoulder and held out his hand. "Brandon Taylor. I'm Charlie's brother."

With Freya settled against him, William held out his free hand. "William Davies. It's nice to meet you."

"Good to meet you." After they shook, Brandon gave a slight wave. "I better be going. I told Mom I'd pick up some ice cream and drop it off on my way home. See you later, Ellie."

He strode off and I turned. Freya, sensing she was no longer the center of attention, began reaching for the rocking toy. William brought her back and tipped it back and forth while Freya giggled. "One more time. We need to go to the store for dinner soon."

I'd left the stroller near the bench, so I used that as an excuse to get myself together. I needed to stop being so nervous! When I turned around, William had Freya on his shoulders while he held her hands, the two of them wearing impossibly large grins. It was the cutest thing I'd seen in a long time and my hormones suddenly went into overdrive. I had this overwhelming urge to have as many babies as I could so I could see that sight again and again. My mind needed to squash that but quick. I didn't even know what was in William's head.

As we headed in the direction of the store, an elderly couple from church passed. Normally, I might have gotten a friendly wave, but today, they waved but also gaped at William. A part of me wanted to sigh. Marysville may have been on the outskirts of a large city, but it was like every other small town. Everyone knew everyone, which meant a man accompanying me to the supermarket as well as holding my daughter would not only prompt a few turned heads but would also bring the inevitable whispers behind the hands of one or two of my mother's gossipy friends. Nothing stayed quiet for long. If William noticed them, he hadn't commented. I also didn't want to spoil the day by pointing it out.

Once we found what we wanted to grill as well as some wine, we checked out and headed home with our purchases riding in Freya's stroller. Home. Where had William planned on staying if he remained in Marysville? Did he plan on relocating here permanently? I'd have to ask him eventually, but I wasn't ready to rock the boat yet. We felt like such a little family right in that moment. I didn't want reality to intrude quite yet.

"Do you need help cooking?"

"No, I'm fine. I thought you'd want to play with Freya. I don't know if she'd want you to help me anyway." I chuckled when I said the last part.

His brows drew down and he frowned. "You aren't upset—"

"No!" Why had I said that? "I'm not. I promise. I want her to know you and for the two of you to have a relationship. I'm happy she's taken to you so quickly. I've never seen her this way."

His face relaxed. "You're sure? I'd thought to take things slow, but when you offered for me to spend the rest of the day with her, I didn't want to pass it up." Something in my chest deflated when he only mentioned Freya.

"I'm positive. You should've been in her life from the beginning, and it seems that she's missed you." I smiled. I wasn't jealous in the slightest other than maybe coveting the attention he was giving my daughter. I wouldn't mind being on the receiving end of a little of that.

Carefully, he pulled her down from his shoulders and kissed her on the forehead. "I'm in her life now. That's all that matters."

The office was closed up when we returned, and everything was quiet. "I think Jena and Charlie have gone out. They were as quiet as church mice earlier, and now, they're not home when they'd normally be rummaging around in the kitchen discussing dinner."

"Charlie introduced herself to me when I came over today. She told me you were in the back yard."

"I hope she was nice. The ladies at church would faint if they heard her speak most of the time. She uses the f-bomb more than the rest of her vocabulary." We carried the food as we went upstairs and set it on the counter. "Jena is the extreme opposite. If she swears, it's bad."

He laughed and set Freya down by her basket of toys near the kitchen. "What about you?"

I peered up toward the ceiling like I was thinking. "I'm probably somewhere in the middle." I loved that rumble he made when I said something funny. It did strange things to my insides just like it had when we first met. Right now, I smiled while I breathed through the somersaults in my stomach.

"Do you think she needs to be changed?" he asked.

"Probably. Do you want me to do it?"

"I do need to learn," he said, picking her back up. "But maybe you should show me just in case I'm all wrong on how I think it should be done."

I pushed his shoulder toward her bedroom. "Come on. It's not rocket science, you know."

Once he put her on the changing pad, I pulled off her little bloomers while he crossed his arms over his chest. "Those don't look like the normal peel and stick types."

"No, they're cloth, with Velcro. It's not that difficult. Did you think I'd clean plastic off the beach on my vacation and use disposables?" I pointed to where I kept the spares on a nearby shelf.

As he handed me the new diaper, he tickled Freya. "I suppose when Mommy puts it that way, it makes perfect sense." Freya giggled. When I had her all done, I picked her up and turned. William held something in his hand, so I stepped closer. He held one of the frames that had rested on the shelf.

"You kept your pictures of us." He turned the photo of us on the sandbank so I could see it.

I leaned my cheek against my daughter's head. "I never deleted any of those photos. I suppose I didn't go through an angry phase like most women. I was depressed and wanted to stop hurting, but I never thought deleting those would help. Once I knew I was pregnant, I saved them for the baby." That was a convenient excuse. I'd saved them as much for me as I had for my daughter. I don't know why I couldn't just say so.

When we returned to the kitchen, we prepped scallops to cook on the grill—I should say I grilled scallops while William played with Freya. She had a great time, and it kept her hands away from the grill, which was a relief. When the girls and I cooked, one of us always remained on duty to keep Freya from getting burned.

We ate at the small table on the balcony, talking mostly about our daughter, but occasionally, other topics came up. William wanted to know what he'd missed—first word, her favorite things. He was as taken with her as she was with him. Not that I could blame him.

I caught Jena sneaking back in while I was cleaning the kitchen. When she saw me, she walked over and leaned against the counter, one eyebrow arched. "How'd it go?"

"It was nice. He spent the day, we had dinner together, and we just finished giving Freya her bath."

"It takes both of you?"

I shrugged. "William's not used to taking care of Freya so he asked me to help. We needed two sets of eyes, however, to make sure we washed all of the macaroni and cheese out of her hair." Jena smiled. She was well aware of how messy Freya could be when she ate. "He's dressing her in the sleeper I put out as we speak."

Her eyes widened and she peeked over her shoulder toward my room. "He's still here?"

"Yes, I hope it's okay."

"Of course it is. I'm sure he wants to spend as much time as possible with his daughter." She skirted around me and pulled a bottle of wine from the wine rack with two glasses. "Charlie and I are going to sit outside and talk for a while."

"You don't have to make yourself scarce, you know." I finished drying the counter and hung the towel over the oven door.

"Ellie, the three of you could use some time without distractions. If that means I sit outside and enjoy the cool weather with a glass of wine, then I'm sure I can survive. Charlie and I can always watch a movie upstairs if we want." She hugged me and took my hand when she pulled back. "He loves you, you know. I may not know him well but Charlie and

I caught a glimpse of y'all in the park. You laughed and he couldn't look away. I'd be willing to bet the only thing that could distract him from you is his daughter. I don't want to be in the way—"

"You're not in the way," I said, insistent.

"Grasp your happiness. I think you have more than a chance if you don't let anything stand in the way. First things first, though. You have to forgive him."

I waved a hand in front of me. "I forgave him a long time ago, but I was afraid to trust him. I've never hurt that way, Jena. I couldn't go through it again, even if it killed me not to call him. Does that make sense?"

"Yes, it does." She pointed toward the door. "I'm going out with Charlie. I'll see you in the morning."

After Jena shut the door, William emerged from my room. He walked a bit stiffly, shoving his hands in his pockets as he drew closer. "She didn't take long to fall asleep."

"Depends on her mood. She had a busy evening. I'm sure it wore her out." I tried to keep my voice upbeat, but without Freya, the air had thickened become awkward. It made it difficult to relax.

He pointed his thumb over his shoulder. "I should go. Thank you for today. I appreciate it."

"You're welcome. Any time."

He cleared his throat. "If I wanted to spend more time with her tomorrow, would that be okay?"

"Yes, of course," I said. "We're all usually up by eight and down in the office by nine. You're welcome whenever."

"Thank you." William nodded. "I'll see you tomorrow." With a small wave, he headed down the stairs.

"Good night." I don't think he heard me. The door closed a minute later.

Chapter 17

Sunday, almost a week later...

I rubbed my eye as I opened a cabinet, all bleary-eyed from the early hour. I'd only been in the kitchen for a moment when a knock came from the balcony. After I started, I headed over to the alarm and pressed the code. Only one person would come over before Freya woke. When I opened the door, William wore a tight smile. "I hope I'm not too early."

"No, Freya should be awake soon. Why don't you come in?" I tucked my hair behind my ear and pressed my hand to my stomach as I made enough room for him to step through. Hopefully, he wouldn't be turned off by my comfy pajamas. The weather cooled a bit the night before and while not attractive, the pants were cozy and warm.

When he stepped inside, he held a tray of cups in his hand.

"Did you stop for coffee?"

"Yes, yours is the one with the 'E' on the side."

As I swiftly closed the door behind him, the smell of my favorite addiction pulled me behind him to the kitchen where he handed me my cup. Before I took a sip, I lifted my eyebrow as I gave him a slight smile. "I hope you know I would've made you coffee."

He ran a hand through his hair. "My dad and I stayed up late talking. This morning, I thought the sooner the better as far as getting some caffeine on board."

My first sip smoothly slid down my throat, providing that dose of warm and fuzzy comfort I craved while I set my cup on the counter. "Breakfast, then? I have some bagels in the freezer, or I can make some eggs. Freya won't wake up for at least another hour."

If only my caffeine fix could cure the unease between me and William! The past week could only have been compared to a roller coaster ride. We had moments where everything clicked and went smoothly and other times where the air between us was heavy and awkward—this was one of those times. The one constant was that William never failed to arrive on the doorstep each morning to spend time with Freya. He spent all day every day at my house, working at the kitchen table during her nap, and left after she fell asleep each night. I adored his manner with our daughter. I just wished I hadn't ruined what originally existed between us. Regardless of what Jena claimed, I couldn't imagine him forgiving me. Too much had happened. We'd both made too many mistakes.

He held up a paper bag. "I brought pastries. Do you still like pain au chocolat?"

I chuckled but the sound wasn't quite right. "I do. Not much gets in the way of chocolate."

"Except coffee maybe." One side of his lips twitched.

"Or you could combine them and make it that much better."

He laughed in that low tone I adored. "Why don't you sit down with me?"

I took the chair across the table as he opened the box from the bakery down the street. He handed me a napkin, and I took a flaky chocolate croissant from its paper nest. When I took a bite, my eyes all but rolled back in my head as the buttery pastry and chocolate melted on my tongue.

"Some things never change," he said.

With a shrug, I took a sip of my coffee and swallowed. "I believe I've grown up a lot, but other than that, very little has changed."

"You have Freya."

I couldn't help but smile like I always had when someone mentioned my daughter. "Freya is an addition—the icing on the cake. She makes me better."

He cleared his throat while he picked at his own breakfast. "You don't have any regrets?"

With a sigh, I shrugged. "I wouldn't be human if I didn't. I could never regret Freya, though. There was never any question of whether or not I should keep her." He glanced up, and if I could've held my breath, I would've. "She was all I had left of you." My eyes burned and I blinked. If I wanted William, Freya, and I to be a family, I had to jump off that cliff at some point to make sure he knew what he meant to me, what he still meant to me. I took another drink of my coffee while I tried not to cry.

"What do you usually do on Sundays?" When I looked up, those crystal blue eyes latched onto mine.

"We usually go to church with my dad. He likes to take Jena, Freya, and I out for lunch afterward." I swallowed, trying not to stumble over my words. "I know you'd be welcome if you'd like to come."

He gave a slight jump. "You're sure your father wouldn't mind?"

I shook my head. "No. Charlie usually tags along when she doesn't have to go home for a family meal. Besides, I know my dad would love to meet you."

Something in his eyes lit. "You've told him about me?"

"Not so much at first. I found it difficult enough to tell him I was pregnant without going into detail. I told him I intended to raise her on my own, which was my choice. If he questioned it, he never pushed. He watched Freya the day after you came into the office. He could tell something was going on and asked. I told him all about you and what happened."

"And he doesn't want to string me up by the balls?" said William with an incredulous laugh. "I've only known that I'm a father for a week, but I'd be looking to buy a shotgun if it were Freya."

One side of my lips curved upward. "My dad is more of a thinker than a doer. He might give you a hard time today, but he won't attack vital parts of your anatomy. I promise." I couldn't help but grin.

"You think it's funny."

I coughed and straightened. "No, I don't think it's funny at all."

"Liar." His dimple peeked out right before he took a bite of his food.

"Tell you what. If my dad starts behaving completely out of character and threatens your balls or any other vital part of your anatomy. I'll protect you."

His eyebrows shot up, but he definitely smiled while he chewed. With that comment, I'd abandoned subtle, but I wasn't going to repair anything between us without putting myself out there.

Movement out of the corner of my eye caught my attention and I watched Jena tiptoe past my room in the direction of the kitchen. She halted mid-step when she noticed William and me.

"You're decent," I said. "Come get your breakfast." When she stepped closer, my self-conscious sister wasn't wearing makeup. She would probably grab whatever she wanted and make a run for it.

William shoved the tray of coffees over. "I believe you drink caramel latte? You're also welcome to a pastry."

Jena paused once again. "You bought me coffee? You didn't have to."

"I was up early. I've snacked on your food all week. It's the least I can do." He pushed the bag over, and Jena peered inside.

"Chocolate croissants? Those are Ellie's favorite."

Was that a faint tinge of pink in his cheeks or was I imagining things? It might be wishful thinking, but a girl could hope, couldn't she?

As predicted, Jena took her coffee and a yogurt and fled for her room after a quick thank you. We wouldn't see her again until she was fully dressed and ready for church.

"Do you dress up for church?" I looked back at William, who opened his jacket to show the cotton Henley underneath. "I'm afraid I don't wear suits much for work so khakis or jeans and a shirt without a logo are my more common dress clothes."

I couldn't complain. Whenever he walked in front of me with Freya, I had no qualms about staring at how those jeans cupped his assets. "Most people our age wear jeans with a nicer top. You'll fit right in."

William opened his mouth, but before he could say anything, a loud yell that was unmistakably Freya's broke the silence. "Ma, ma, ma, ma!"

I scooted my chair from the table. "Someone's awake." I gave a slight jerk of my head toward Freya's room. "Come on. You can get her ready while I get dressed." I grabbed my coffee and gave him a minute to get up from the table. I had this urge to take his hand, but flirting was a lot different than pushing things physically. What if he rejected the overture?

When we walked into Freya's room, she started bouncing in her crib when she saw William. "Da, da, da, da!"

"Hi, darlin,'" he said. His voice had this sweet drawl, and I had to keep from melting into a puddle on the floor. When he picked her up and cuddled her to his chest, she put her hands on his cheeks and gave him a big open-mouthed kiss on the lips.

I bit my lips to keep from laughing. "I told you she'd be happy to see you."

He wore a wide grin as he wiped his mouth. "What do you want her to wear?"

I pulled her little chocolate brown corduroy jumper with the patchwork owl on it from the closet with her striped tights and her brown Mary Jane's. "If you'll change her diaper, we'll get her breakfast first. Then, you can dress her in this." I set it on her dresser. "She'll smear her food all over her clothes if you get her ready first."

I helped him get her set up for breakfast before I hurried into my bathroom for a quick shower. I put on my blue sweater dress, a pair of dove grey leggings, and my grey boots. When I emerged from the bathroom after fixing my hair and putting on a little makeup, he had Freya all ready to go.

He glanced up from holding Freya's hand and walking her around. "You look nice." It was all I could do to keep my shoulders from drooping. I didn't want to look "nice." I wanted him to compliment me the way he had on the island. Adjectives like lovely, beautiful, or amazing would've been a thousand times better than "nice." Pretty would've been tolerable as well.

"Thank you." I couldn't ignore a compliment—even if it wasn't the type I preferred.

Jena and Charlie were waiting for us in the living room, and we walked down to church like every Sunday when the weather was clear. When we arrived, Charlie joined her family near the front while Jena and I headed for Dad, who, as usual, sat near the back.

When Jena touched his shoulder, he started a bit, stood, and kissed her cheek, but hesitated, glancing behind me before he kissed mine. "Well, who's this?" He held out his hand. "Tom Barrett, Ellie's father."

William held Freya to his side with one arm while he shook my father's hand. "William Davies, sir. It's nice to meet you. Ellie's told me a lot about you."

Dad nodded and shot me a glance. "She's told me a lot about you as well. I'm glad to see you're getting to spend time with my granddaughter." He tickled Freya's belly, making her giggle.

"As much as I can, sir."

Jena entered the pew first with William after, leaving me to sit next to Dad. During the opening hymn, Dad leaned over close to my ear. "Your young man seems pretty uptight."

I turned my head so he could hear me. "He's afraid you might string him up by the balls." I could've sworn I heard my dad snort, but he covered his mouth and coughed. Jena peered over, but after I shrugged like I had no clue, she returned to singing.

"How's it going between the two of you?"

"I'm not sure. He runs warm and then cold."

He took my hand and gave it a squeeze. "If he doesn't give you another chance, it's his loss. I think his willingness to attend church with both you and Freya says something. Don't give up hope yet."

I rubbed my palm down my leg and tried to take a discreet breath to settle in. Just my luck, it was one of those mornings where the service dragged by like it would never end and my butt petrified from sitting in one position for so long. Freya turned restless just after the sermon, but between the four of us, we were able to keep her occupied enough that she hadn't started crying or worse, screaming.

When church ended, my father always enjoyed the social time, so we remained and lingered in the parish hall, which I knew was a bad idea. A couple of the grandmotherly regulars surrounded William, who was still holding Freya, and almost immediately began their inquisition.

I kept an eye on him as I grabbed the two of us coffee. He bore their nosy questions well, but he stood so rigid. Dad was right. He looked uptight, as though he had a poker shoved somewhere uncomfortable. I poured us both cups and hurried over. "Mrs. Abrams, Mrs. Truett, how are you both?" I handed William his cup and smiled.

Mrs. Abrams put a hand to her lower back, and I bit my cheek. "Oh, you know my sciatica always flares when cold weather comes, but my son's coming over later to clean up the yard. It's been an eyesore since that maple in the front lost all its leaves."

"We were just speaking to your young man, Ellie," said Mrs. Truett with a recognizable glint in her eye. She was fishing. "Freya certainly seems taken with him." She touched our daughter's arm, then lifted her eyebrows as she and Mrs. Abrams glanced at one another with identical expressions.

I kept my face as cheerful and neutral as I could. I didn't want to give the old biddies more to talk about than was really there. "Actually, William is Freya's father." Like they couldn't tell by the resemblance! "He lives in Savannah and is staying in Marysville to spend time with her." I'd always been tight-lipped about Freya's father. In a small town where everyone knew everyone else's business, I'd always kept mine to myself until today. Now, they'd be talking for weeks!

"Isn't that lovely." Mrs. Truett twisted the bracelet on her wrist.

"Ellie?" I turned at my dad calling me. "Are you ready? I called over to Harbor View. They have a table on the patio waiting for us."

I looped my arm through William's and hoped like hell he wouldn't reject it. "Looks like we have to go. Have a nice day, ladies.

"I'm sorry about that," I said softly as I pulled him toward Dad. "It's a small town. When people realized I was pregnant, speculation ran rampant about who knocked me up. I refused to confirm or deny anything, so every time I chatted with

Brandon or was seen with a client who wasn't with the bride, the next rumor claimed they were the father. Your appearance will definitely start all that back up again. At least the rumors will be true this time. I hope so anyway."

"It's okay. Small southern towns all resemble each other in that way. If I showed up with you to church in Savannah, we'd have a similar gaggle of old ladies prying and asking us questions."

I took his coffee cup and tossed it in the garbage with my own as we passed. "You seemed uncomfortable."

"I was." He chuckled and shrugged. "They aren't the gossipy ladies I grew up with. I don't have my bearings here. I don't know who the harmless gossips are and which ones are out for blood."

"Those two are friends with my mom. They'd normally be harmless, but they'll run right back and tell my mother everything. That's what makes them a problem." Did he remember my relationship with my mother? I really didn't want to explain that all again if I could help it.

"I can see why you wouldn't trust them." His eyes met mine and we had our least awkward interaction of that morning. How I hoped the ease between us would continue!

We walked back to the house and piled into my car for the drive to the restaurant. We'd known the owner for as long as I could remember, so like Dad said, a table on the enclosed porch awaited us when we arrived.

My dad didn't treat William any differently than anyone else, and eventually, William's shoulders relaxed and he began to take part in the conversation rather than concentrating completely on Freya. By the time we finished eating, we seemed like any normal family out for Sunday brunch. We'd laughed and discussed our plans for the week—Dad even asked William about his business.

When Freya decided she was done with her food, Jena and I took her to the ladies' room to clean her up. On our way back, I grabbed Jena's arm at the sound of Dad's voice. "Now that you're divorced, do you intend to pursue my daughter?" Jena turned to me with an exaggerated grimace while I winced.

I closed my eyes and held in a groan. Dad! What was he doing?

"I'm not completely certain, sir. I'm just trying to bond with my daughter and do what's best for her." I closed my eyes and held Freya a bit tighter. William's voice wasn't the easy tone he'd had during the meal. I didn't want our interactions stilted and uncomfortable anymore. Hopefully, this wouldn't make things worse between us.

"You don't think you and Ellie together is best for her?"

"With all due respect, sir, whether your daughter and I decide to pursue a relationship is between us." William's tone remained respectful but firm. My dad wouldn't respect William if he backed down. It was good he held his ground.

"You've both hurt one another," said Dad, "but I think the two of you have a chance. My daughter wouldn't have been so hurt if she didn't love you deeply. I'd like to see both of you happy. Don't pass up the chance to be with the right person. I married the wrong woman, as I believe you have done also. Neither of us can get those years back. I'm thankful Jena and Ellie came from my marriage or the time would've been completely lost. You've corrected your mistake. Now, you need to—"

"We're back!" I cringed. The words came out too cheerful and too loudly. I just needed to make Dad stop. He meant well, but I didn't want to force William to be with me if he didn't want to try.

"I think we're ready to go." Dad stood and pushed his chair under the table. "I told Charlie's father I'd come over for the football game this afternoon. I'd offer for you to come, William, but I'm sure you'd prefer to spend the day with the ladies."

If only the ground would swallow me whole. Why did he suddenly have the need to embarrass me? On the way home, I sat in the back with Freya and Jena while Dad asked William a million more questions about his company. Freya was asleep by the time we returned, so I tucked her into her bed and carefully closed the door behind me. William sat in the living room, having taken the opportunity to call his father.

"Yes, I will . . . yes, sir . . . yes, sir . . . goodbye." He looked up at me when I entered. "He wanted me to tell you 'Hello.'"

"How is your father?" I sat down on the other side of the sofa.

"He's fine."

"He seems nice."

A side of his lips quirked upward. "Yours is protective of you."

"I overheard on my way back from the bathroom. I'm sorry he butted in. I would never want you to feel obligated because of Freya." I couldn't stop trembling. A lot could be riding on what I said, not to mention his response. "You'll always be her father, no matter what."

He nodded almost absently until his eyes latched onto the framed maternity photo of me on the end table. "You had pictures taken on the beach?"

"I have a lot of photos. Micah and I have been friends since high school, and he's the photographer for most of our weddings. He took the pictures as a thank you, but he also used the photos for his portfolio. He doesn't shoot many maternity albums."

"It's nice. You didn't have this one in the album you gave me."

"No, that book is great for keeping Freya busy sometimes. She loves to look at the pictures of herself, but she's too young to understand she's in my tummy in those."

He picked up the frame and stared at it. "Was she active when you were pregnant?"

"She moved a good bit. I don't know that it was more than any other baby, but she did keep me awake some nights with her rolling around."

"Who was there for you when she was born?" His voice sounded a little raspy.

I curled my legs up on the sofa, my elbow propped on the back and my chin in my hand. "Jena and Charlie both acted as Lamaze coaches. I'm still in shock that Charlie didn't pass out. I really thought she wouldn't make it. From the moment the first contractions woke me up, the entire process felt like forever, but compared to other women I've spoken to, it was really very short. Once I began progressing, everything moved fairly quickly, but I walked as much as I could to speed things along."

I told him about Freya's birth from the first contraction until our discharge from the hospital. I pulled out my laptop and showed him a few videos from just after she was born. He listened quietly without his attention drifting. His eyes either remained on my face, on a photo, if I had one to show him, or the videos. We talked and I told him stories about Freya until she woke a couple of hours later. As awkward as the morning had been, Dad's nosy intentions hadn't caused a return of the uneasiness. The afternoon was nice.

I scanned the kitchen. Everything was cleaned and put away, the sun had already set, and on the balcony, the lit solar lanterns were visible through the draperies. Where were Freya and William? He'd taken Freya for a bath while I loaded the dishwasher and might have tried to rock her once she was dressed for bed. When she wasn't eating her snack and dinner, Freya had played all evening long and had a thoroughly wonderful time. She'd been so tired during her bath, William had called me in so we could chuckle at the heaviness of our daughter's eyes.

I padded along the carpet runner in the hall until I reached the door of my room where I stopped dead in my tracks. There, on the bed, was William fast asleep with Freya sprawled across his chest, her mouth open and drool dribbling down her cheek.

If that sight wouldn't send a woman's ovaries into overdrive, I didn't know what would. I tiptoed out and fetched my phone. Once I'd made sure it was on silent, I took several photos of the two of them.

From experience, I knew sleeping with her like that was not comfortable at all. I also didn't want Freya to fall out of bed, so carefully, one arm at a time, I freed Freya from his hold. She didn't stir when I lifted her or when I laid her in her crib. Instead, she sighed and rolled to her side, cuddled to her raccoon.

Despite the quiet afternoon at home, I was tired. It was earlier than I usually went to sleep, but if I was grumpy tomorrow, Jena and Charlie wouldn't be as patient as they had been a week ago. I changed into my pajamas then found myself staring at William in my bed. Should I sleep with Jena, or would he care if I shared with him?

When I fell asleep on the sofa or somewhere other than my bed, I never slept well. William could hardly be angry with me when he'd already made himself comfortable in my bed, could he?

Oh, screw it! I pulled back the covers and slipped inside, trying not to shift the mattress. The edge dug into my leg as I curled up so I moved around trying to get comfortable. At some point, I suppose I relaxed because the next thing I knew, the morning sun filtered through the sheers in my bedroom, and I had a familiar weight over my waist and someone breathing steadily in my ear.

Chapter 18

The arm around my waist tugged me closer, and I closed my eyes, savoring the warmth of his solid chest pressing against my back. It'd been so long since William held me, and I wanted to live in the moment. It'd been too long! His breathing changed and the hand resting against my stomach shifted, his thumb tracing along the lower edge of my ribs before his arm began a slow and careful retreat.

Jena had told me to grasp my happiness, but could I muster the courage to face him? I'd need to bite the bullet eventually and now was as good a time as any, wasn't it? As his fingers skimmed my side, I held my breath and rolled to my back, my eyes meeting his. "Good morning," I whispered since I didn't want to wake Freya.

He softly cleared his throat. "Good morning. I hope I didn't make you uncomfortable." I loved the way he looked when he first woke up, his curls sticking out at odd angles and all adorably mussed. I especially adored that his first thing in the morning look hadn't changed at all in the past two years.

"No, I've missed this," I said, shifting to my side so that I faced him. "I've missed you." We lay close together, our heads only separated by the break in the pillows. "I hope you don't mind that I crept into bed with you last night." My cheeks burned like I was sitting in front of a roaring fire. Could I have sounded any more desperate?

"I fell asleep in your bed. If you'd wanted, you could have woken me up and kicked me out. I certainly wouldn't expect you to spend the night on the sofa." He lifted one of the curls along my shoulder and wound it around his finger. "Do you remember when we used to talk like this?"

The memory brought a smile to my face. "Yes, how could I forget? We spent hours sharing tales of our childhoods, and you telling me about your mom. You'd told me so many stories about her, I'd felt like I'd met her in person"

He nestled into the pillow as his eyes met mine again. "Is that why you named Freya after her?"

I held my breath, reached out, and smoothed a few creases in his shirt. "I think I was looking for some connection to you. Because of South Carolina law, I couldn't put your name on the birth certificate. She couldn't bear your last name without your consent. Naming her after your mother was how I attached her to you without you actually claiming her. Now that you're here, we can go to the county health department and you can fill out the forms to add your name to her birth certificate."

Blinking rapidly, he nodded, his eyes on where he still played with my hair. "I'd like to do that as soon as possible. Whenever you can get away from work."

"I have some accounts to update this morning, but I do need to make a trip in that direction later today. We could go then if you want?"

"Does Freya ever go to daycare while you work?"

"No, she's never needed to. When I discovered I was pregnant, Jena, Charlie, and I hashed out how we would cover my accounts at work and made plans for as much as we could before she came—of course, nothing was as simple as we thought it would be, but we still never considered daycare an option. We were willing to work together and we learned how to manage. When Freya was first born, I took her nearly everywhere except for weddings. She kept a pretty routine schedule with naps and nursing. We made sure the clients knew Charlie and I were a team on my accounts since Charlie needed to cover those events on the wedding day. I breastfed, and Freya adamantly refused to take a bottle, so I couldn't be replaced. In my office, I set up a bassinet and a swing. Those have evolved to a table and toys. I take time out to play with her, and I work to get as much done during her nap as I can. Charlie and Jena move the toys and table into their offices if I need to go out, and they'll watch her. Some days, my dad comes over and will spend a morning or an afternoon with her."

William glanced over my shoulder toward Freya's crib before his eyes latched onto mine. "You've done an amazing job with her. She's happy and confident and knows she's loved. It's obvious in how she interacts with you." His eyes held mine so steadily. I couldn't doubt that he meant it. "She's fortunate to have you for her mother."

"Thank you," I whispered.

His fingers trailed a line of heat down my cheek, and I couldn't look away as his face drew closer and closer. When his lips finally pressed against mine, my insides turned into a tingly, churning mess of butterflies and flips, and even though my eyes were closed, they burned like I needed to cry. How did this man do this to me?

"Mama!"

I couldn't help it. I started to laugh and his shoulders shook as he pulled away.

"Da da!"

"Does she always have such impeccable timing?"

I stretched my legs toward the foot of the bed. "I don't know. This is the first time she's ever interrupted something." I stretched my arms over my head and closed my eyes, relishing the satisfying pull of my muscles when something just barely brushed the flesh to the inside of my hipbone. My eyes opened and I lifted my head as William's fingertips caressed along the three faint lines on my right hip revealed by the low waistline of my pajama pants and my top riding up. "They're from when she dropped about a week before she was born. I'd managed to go the entire pregnancy without stretch marks, and she managed to squeeze those in right at the end."

I was paralyzed when he bent over and kissed the white lines that I'd grown to accept would be a part of my body forever. Few women treasured those scars; however, mine weren't bad when you considered how many stretch marks some women possessed. At that moment, however, I would've accepted scars from head to toe if he'd press his lips against each one of them so tenderly. Goosebumps peppered my flesh and parts of me sprang to life that I'd suppressed since I'd left the island. How did they begin to ache so intensely with a mere two or three kisses? My thighs clenched together as I remembered his lips trailing lower; how my back arched off the bed at the pleasure he gave me.

"Da, da, da, da!"

His dimples were on full display when he scooted from the bed and walked into Freya's room. "Good morning, sweet pea." How could he seem so unaffected when I was melting like a popsicle on a hot summer day? "I hope you slept well."

The rustling of fabric was enough to let me know he was changing her diaper, so I got up and did what I needed to in the bathroom. When I was done, I opened the door and dug a spare toothbrush from a drawer, putting it on the counter as he walked in.

"I have a toothbrush for you if you need it." I held out my hands to Freya. "Let's brush your teeth." I had an extra soft toddler's toothbrush and toothpaste that I lightly ran over her teeth while William watched. She grinned larger than normal when we were done, showing him her teeth.

"They look beautiful," he said with a massive smile. "Do you want to watch Daddy brush his?"

She watched him happily so he started, making silly faces that made her giggle. He then held her so I could brush mine.

"I love this." He cuddled Freya to his chest, nuzzling his nose in her hair. "I know it probably seems ridiculous, but I don't even want to go back to the hotel to change clothes."

"Why don't you pack up your belongings and bring them here?" It was an impulsive offer. Would Jena care? So far, she'd been encouraging and supportive. I hoped that wouldn't change.

"What about Jena and Charlie?"

"Charlie has her own apartment upstairs, and Jena told me to grasp my happiness. I could ask her if you want, but I think she'll be fine with it. I don't know how long you plan to remain in town, but all of that time in The Magnolia is going to get expensive."

He looked at Freya. "I'm not worried about how much it costs. I just want to spend time with her." My stomach sank a little. He finally seemed interested in me—appeared to have forgiven me, but for once, I'd have liked him to include me.

"Jena understands that, which is why I know she'd offer if it were her." My eyes blurred a little with tears. I needed to get away from him before I made a complete ninny of myself.

When I reached the door, I was drawn back by my hand. "Elle? What's wrong?"

"Nothing." I didn't want to tell him I was a selfish cow. "It's understandable you'd want to spend as much time with Freya as possible."

His eyes searched mine and the next thing I knew, his free hand cupped my cheek. "I know I've been standoffish this week. One day, we'd get along great and everything would seem perfect—too perfect. Then, I'd think about how you didn't tell me about Freya, which would make me angry and wonder if we could really work things out between us. The problem or the solution, depending upon how you look at it, is that my heart wants you and no one else will suffice. So, don't doubt that I want to be with you. I do still love you."

"You do?" Why did my voice have to be so needy and pathetic?

He nodded softly. "Yeah, I do. I was mad at you, but I didn't stop loving you. I want to be with both of you. Don't ever doubt it."

My eyes searched his, verifying what he said was true. "You were so angry. I've hoped if I gave you some time you'd forgive me. I feared you wouldn't.

His hand squeezed mine. "My dad has made sure to remind me on more than one occasion how badly I screwed up when we first got involved. You had every right not to trust me. He made sure to inform me how we both made mistakes but that I needed to choose whether I wanted you or whether I wanted to hold onto my anger. He made sure to include that in the end, my anger wouldn't make me happy."

One side of my lips tugged upwards. "My dad didn't quite say it that way. He said we'd both made mistakes and told me to give you time."

William tugged me closer. "Yours did say much the same to me. I suppose we both have our fathers to thank."

I rolled my eyes. "Don't give mine too much credit. I'd like to think we'd have figured it out on our own . . . eventually."

Those dimples I adored appeared as he brought me to him and hugged me, his lips grazing my temple. "I do want to go slower this time," he said softly by my ear. "We need to build that trust between us again. I don't think another ten-day whirlwind romance would be the best way to accomplish that. What about you?"

I laughed and shook my head, not ready to let go of him quite yet.

He let out a heavy breath. "I should go to the hotel and pack up my luggage so I can bring it here. Then, I can spend the morning with Freya while you work." He drew back and brushed my hair behind my ear. "When did you want to go to the health department to submit that paperwork?"

"The best time would be while she takes her nap. Jena and Charlie will be here if she wakes up earlier than usual. Otherwise, she'd get bored and fussy while we took care of that business."

He handed Freya to me but held us both while he rubbed our daughter's back. "Then I'd better get going. I won't be long. Do you need me to stop by the store for anything?"

"Not unless you need something in particular. We keep eggs, bread, yogurt, and fruit for breakfast."

"I'm sure there's plenty of coffee too."

I pinched his side. "There's always coffee."

"You're such a coffee addict. How did you survive being pregnant?" he said, taking Freya back from me and lifting her over his head.

"I got used to decaf. The day she was finally weaned, I had the jitters all day long because I wasn't accustomed to the caffeine anymore."

He passed our daughter back, kissing her again on the forehead. "I'm really going this time." After one last wave, he walked through the door, his footsteps padding along the wood floor. He'd left his shoes by the stairs last night since we didn't wear them upstairs.

After I took care of Freya's morning routine, we ate breakfast. Jena came downstairs from her bedroom right about the time we'd finished. "Did I hear William leaving early this morning?" Her eyebrows were lifted on her forehead and her lips were pressed together. The little witch was trying not to smile.

"He fell asleep holding Freya last night. I didn't wake him." I watched Freya pick up a handful of scrambled eggs and shove them into her mouth with her little fist. "I hope you don't mind. I told him he could stay here rather than The Magnolia. He was concerned about how you'd feel, but I hoped you'd be okay with it."

My sister sat down across from me with her yogurt. "He's more than welcome to stay here. I hope you didn't think I'd say no."

"No, I was certain you'd agree," I said, "but I still wanted to make sure."

"The two of you have jumped back into things very quickly." I recognized that tone. She wasn't disapproving, only concerned.

"I know it doesn't seem like it since we slept in the same bed, but we plan on taking things slowly. He's kissed me. Nothing else has happened." Was I defending myself or him? We were consenting adults, after all.

"Don't get defensive. I don't want you to get hurt. I remember what you were like when you got off that plane."

"I'd like to think we've both grown up since then. We both know what we want."

"Good. I want you to be happy."

Freya opened her mouth and said, "Aah!" at Jena who laughed and gave her a small spoonful of her yogurt.

When she was finished eating, I put out some toys so Freya could play on the bathmat while I took a quick shower. I fussed over my hair more than usual then put on my new cream dress and boots. The cooler weather this week allowed me to wear a few new outfits I'd bought on clearance in the spring. Freya'd followed me from the bathroom and pulled my shoes out of the closet, putting them on and attempting to walk in them. She was definitely my daughter. That child loved shoes.

I was putting on my last earring when someone knocked on my bedroom door. "What's up?"

The door cracked, and William poked his head through. "Can I come in?"

I chuckled. "Sorry, I thought it was Jena." I waved him inside. "Yes, absolutely."

He wheeled his suitcase through the door. "Where do you want me to put this?"

"Da da?" Freya walked toward him in a pair of boots that reached her thighs.

"Hi, pumpkin," he said, picking her up while he chuckled. "I can't believe she's calling me that so fast." The boots fell from her feet which made her reach for them and wiggle to get down.

"She's said it for a while in babbles, but I made sure to call you Daddy as much as possible since that day in the back yard. I guess she caught on pretty quickly."

"Thank you." He set her down and she dropped to her rear on the floor, immediately pulling the boots back on her feet while I opened the doors to my closet.

"Why don't you unpack? We have a room downstairs where we've stored the furniture Jena and I didn't need when we moved in. We could put your suitcase there for now."

He pulled his luggage closer. "Sounds good." His gaze drifted down to my feet and back up. "You look amazing. You told me on the island how you loved dresses. Do you wear them every day?"

"Pretty much. Jena and Charlie tend to wear classy pant outfits and occasionally skirts. I have a few skirts but I prefer dresses."

He shoved his hands in his pockets and looked down to his feet before his eyes met mine again. "You wore a lot of dresses on the island. I always thought you looked so feminine and pretty." His face suddenly seemed redder than it had before. "They also show off your legs, which I can't complain about."

I put my finger over his lips to stop him before I was tempted to spend the day with him instead of planning weddings. "I have to get to work, and our daughter is right over there. If you need anything or have a question, I'll be downstairs. I'll be back up around noon to help you with Freya's lunch."

He nodded and smiled under my finger. That incorrigible, wicked grin made cake orders and flower selections the last thing I wanted to do today. Before I could think too much about it, I kissed Freya and hauled butt to my office.

I'd love to say the morning passed quickly, but by noon, I felt like it'd been a week. I suppose that happens when you'd rather be doing something else. With that said, I did get a lot done and had not only finally caught up from the day I took off the week before, but also made good headway on several accounts.

When I joined William and Freya, he was sitting on the sofa reading her a book while she hugged her raccoon tightly. I fixed lunch for her, and once she'd eaten, she fell asleep in no time, leaving William and I free to run errands. The problem was that Jena's office door was closed and Charlie wasn't to be found.

"Maggie?" Our assistant looked up from her computer. "Is Jena in a meeting?"

"She and Charlie are in with a new client, a walk-in, who came in about ten minutes ago." She glanced at the baby monitor in my hand. "Do you need to go? I can keep an ear out for Freya until Jena and Charlie are free."

"That would be amazing. Thank you. She just fell asleep. She should be fine for a couple of hours. I have my cell if you need me."

"Don't worry about a thing." She took the handset and placed it on her desk. "We'll be here when you get back."

William was oddly quiet on the trip to the health department, which made my back and neck tense. Was he having doubts, or was he simply upset he had to claim his own daughter? Maybe I was just being paranoid? I pulled into the parking space and turned off the car. "Is something wrong?"

"Nothing." He shook his head and rubbed his hands up and down his thighs. "It's all kind of overwhelming. I have a daughter and we're making it official. All I have to do is sign a piece of paper and I'm a father."

I took his hand in mine. "You were a father before. This is nothing more than a formality."

He squeezed my hand and smiled. "When you put it that way, I suppose you're right. Let's go."

Chapter 19

My eyes blinked at the bright glare of sunlight filtering in through the sheers. With a sigh, I looked at the clock, waiting a second for the numbers to come into focus, before turning back to stare at the clean, white ceiling with a noisy exhale. Why was I awake at six on a Saturday morning? I should still be fast asleep with William curled up to my side, his hand resting on my stomach. Just like he was at this moment.

It'd been a month since we'd made that trip to the health department. After I'd made several stops for work, he'd insisted on taking me to lunch to celebrate the occasion. He'd been a smiling fool for the rest of the day, but it'd been the greatest sight ever. I'd been such a bitch to keep Freya from him for so long. That evening, he'd walked to the store to grab some supplies for dinner and surprised us by bringing home not only flowers for me, but also a bouquet for Jena and Charlie, too, claiming he owed them. They'd been there for me and Freya when he wasn't.

I rolled to my side and curled into him, his arm wrapping around my back and cuddling me closer. "What's wrong?" he said in a low murmur.

"Nothing, I just woke up earlier than I wanted."

"Mmm . . . Go back to sleep."

The scent of him filled my nostrils, and I breathed deeply the remnants of his cologne mixed with whatever it was that was all William. For the last month, he'd held my hand when he could spare one from Freya and gave me fairly chaste kisses that reminded me of what I'd already had and missed desperately. He never tried for more, but Lord, I wanted him to! We planned on building our relationship back up slowly, but frankly, going slow was for sissies. I wanted more than a tame peck and teenager-worthy hand holding.

My lips reached for that little spot of flesh at the base of his neck. The one that always made him groan like he was in pain. I kissed it, suckling just a little before doing it again. My teeth grazed along the taut skin as his fingers dug into my back.

"Elle," he said all low, hoarse, and sexy as hell. "What are you doing?"

I took his response as one of approval and shifted closer, sliding my knee up along his leg. "What does it feel like I'm doing?" At least one part of him wanted me since he was standing at attention and pressing insistently against my hip.

"I thought we were taking things slowly." His head lifted a little giving me more access so I could graze my teeth along his earlobe.

At his rumbling growl, I grinned. "There's slow and there's a snail's pace."

"You're driving me crazy." His voice oozed out all thick and gravelly, warming my insides like a sip of fine scotch.

I gave a breathy chuckle and ran my hand down his chest, letting it snake around his waist to cup his rear. "Good, you've been driving me crazy for weeks."

His fingers threaded through my hair and tightened as he pulled me in for a searing kiss, his tongue finally taking the plunge and caressing mine. I'd forgotten how well he could kiss—how his soft lips cradled mine just so and he used his tongue in teasing tastes. I could kiss him for hours and never tire of it.

He rolled me under him as my legs rose up to cradle his hips between my thighs, but he didn't stop kissing me. I coasted my fingers along his waistline, his answering shiver letting on how much I affected him.

We kissed until my jaw ached. Then, he began trailing his lips along my jawline. A shudder coursed through my body when he bit lightly at the base of my neck. I loved being so close to him, but I wanted more. My hands cupped his ass as I ground against him. "Will," I said. "Please."

He froze and lifted up with his forehead furrowed in this adorable frown. "What about Freya?"

Had he lost his mind? She was asleep and would be for another hour. "She's still out like a light. She won't know."

He pecked me on the lips, jumped up from the bed, and carefully closed the doors between our room and hers. "I'm sorry, but I can't when she might wake up and hear us or, God forbid, see us."

His cheeks held faint tinges of a blush, and I laughed as he took two more steps and dropped on top of me with an "umph," his arms absorbing most of his weight.

My top was pulled off and thrown somewhere so his fingertips could trace the valley between my breasts. They made circles around each one, teasing me mercilessly before he finally took my nipple in his mouth. Our eyes held while he suckled, and I became more and more impatient for him to get to the main event. I enjoyed foreplay, and he was definitely a master, but it'd been two years. Two years!

When I couldn't take it anymore, I pushed him to his knees and dragged his pajama bottoms over his hips, taking what I wanted firmly in my hand and stroking from base to tip.

William collapsed back onto his feet when my thumb found a tiny droplet at the tip and swirled it around the head.

He grabbed my hand. "You have to stop. I can't . . . It's been too long." He pressed me back into the mattress and my own pajama bottoms made a noise like they tore, they were removed so quickly. When he covered me with his body, he kissed me deeply then sucked in a deep breath. "Condom. We need a condom."

"I have condoms in the bedside table, but I'm on the pill this time." I conveniently left out that Charlie gave me the condoms a few weeks ago "just in case." "I haven't been with anyone since you on the island, and they tested me when I was pregnant with Freya."

"Are you sure?" He cleared his throat while he brushed a few curls from my face. "I haven't been with anyone else either."

I nodded while I traced my fingertips down his sides. "I'm sure. The condoms didn't work that well anyway."

His low laugh made my tummy tremble as he lowered and claimed my lips again. When he finally slid home where he belonged, it was all I could do not to cry. God, I remembered how incredible it felt to have him sheathed inside me, filling me, my hips thrusting to take him as deep as he could reach.

A delicious heat bloomed in my lower belly and coiled tighter and tighter. William whispered my name and buried his head in my neck while both of us panted and our breaths became increasingly erratic.

He moaned and gripped my hips tighter. "I'm not going to last. It's been too long and you feel too good."

"It's okay. I have a funny feeling we'll do this again."

His fingers slid down my stomach until they massaged that spot just above where we were joined, building that spiraling tension to an unbearable peak that made me shatter and call out his name. He followed me with a loud groan, collapsing heavily on top of me.

"Lord, I love you, Elle." He breathed like he'd run a race, his quick exhales creating a warmth that pebbled my flesh. "I should've been saying it for the last few weeks, but I kept convincing myself you weren't ready to hear it. I love you. Since the island, it's always been you. I couldn't imagine anyone else and it wouldn't have been fair to even try. They would've been compared to an impossible standard."

Tears flooded my eyes, and I drew his face up to mine. "I love you too. I've never felt for someone else what I feel for you." Our lips met and he rolled us to our sides, wiping away the tear that had fallen to my cheek with his hand.

"I wanted to give you time to trust me again," he said softly.

"And I love you for it, but I've been with you before. I knew what I was missing."

His deep laugh settled into my heart. "So, you were horny."

I rolled my eyes pinched him.

"Ow," he said, sliding his hand up my side.

"Don't tickle me." I grabbed his hand and laced my fingers with his. "You have to understand. In those months after the island, I almost couldn't breathe through the pain. I had to pick myself up and keep going, not just for myself, but for Freya. I didn't stay away just because I was afraid to trust you, but also because I couldn't ever go through that again.

When you showed up in my office, I decided to suck it up and go for it. It wasn't fair to keep Freya's existence from you and I still missed you."

His eyes held mine. "You don't know how badly I wanted to come here and beg you to take me back."

"Probably just as many times as I thought about finding you in Savannah and telling you about Freya."

He sighed and touched his forehead to mine. "Speaking of Savannah, I have business I need to handle at the office, but I don't want to leave the two of you. The trip would only be overnight, but I've missed so much—"

"We could go with you." I didn't require convincing. He'd given up so much to be with us. It was the least I could do.

His head jerked back. "Really? You'd go?"

"You stay here to be near our daughter."

"And you," he said softly, squeezing my hand.

"And me." I couldn't help but smile. "I don't see why we can't give up a day or two so you can do your job?"

"Dad and I are in the process of setting up the Savannah office so we can both move permanently to the Charleston area. I have an assistant in the home office who's more than capable of handling the job and wants the promotion. I only need to tie up a few loose ends and sell my house. Dad, of course, needs to find a place to live here first."

"You'd move here for us? Your life has always been in Savannah."

"You and Freya are my life." The arm around me drew me tighter to him while my eyes began to burn like crazy. "My company operates out of three states. I can live nearby and still easily run everything."

"Would you buy your own house here?" I didn't want him to have his own place. I wanted him to continue playing house with us.

His finger lifted my chin so I could see his face. "That depends on you. If you want me to stay with you, I'd be more than happy to live in this house, or we could buy our own place and leave this one for Jena. It's up to you."

My stomach had tightened when I asked the question but relaxed when he said he'd be willing to stay. "I want us to be together," I said. "I know it's fast when we said we'd go slowly, but I don't want you to go anywhere."

"I could buy a house for the three of us?"

"I know you could, but maybe we should keep an eye out for something we love. I'd rather stay in Marysville. I like walking nearly everywhere and being so close to where I work."

"We could do that. I'm just thinking ahead. We should talk to a real estate agent who can search for a place for Dad and also keep an ear to the ground for something for us."

"Jena has a friend who found this house for us. While I speak to her about our trip to Savannah, I'll get his phone number. I'm all caught up unless someone changes details on their weddings, and the girls have my cell phone number if they need me."

His index finger trailed down my chest, between my breasts, and to my stomach where he pressed his palm to my bellybutton and pushed me to my back. "Enough seriousness. I have a rather dismal performance to make up for."

"I didn't find it dismal, but who am I to object if you wish to improve?"

He laughed as he crawled over me, depositing a soft kiss by my navel before searing my skin with a much hotter and wetter kiss on my side. My body, which had been wonderfully satiated, suddenly sprang back to life as my heart started to quicken.

After we made love for a second time, we showered together, still kissing and teasing one another while we bathed each other more thoroughly than necessary. Freya was babbling in her crib when I got out, so I put on some pajamas and changed her diaper while William shaved and dressed for the day.

Jena was already in the kitchen when I walked in but didn't say anything until I had Freya strapped in her seat and was searching the fridge.

"I forgot to mention it earlier, but the woman who's been renting the garage apartment gave me notice last month."

"She did?" I straightened and looked at Jena over the refrigerator door. That apartment had made things very cushy financially for us the last two years. I hated to lose the extra money. "Have you advertised for a new tenant yet?"

"I haven't because I've been thinking about moving in."

I shut the refrigerator, grabbed a banana, and began slicing it onto Freya's tray. "But you have a place to live here."

She walked over and leaned against the counter, taking my hand. "Ellie, I love you and I've loved living here with you and Freya."

"But," I said, lifting my eyebrows. It was obvious that word was coming.

"*But*, William is back in your life and you and Freya are both so happy he's here. I think the three of you should have some time on your own to be a family. I'm not saying you can't do that with me living here, but I think it would be better for y'all if I go."

I hated this. This was just as much her home as mine. I didn't want her to feel like she had to leave. "Are you sure you don't want us to move into the apartment? This is your home too. Neither of us minds you living here, you know."

"I do know that. This isn't a spur of the moment decision. I've thought about it for a while, and I'm actually excited to move. I can finally use my furniture that's been in storage downstairs and you can move what's yours up here. If William has a desk, he can put it into the old storage room and have his own office space until he finds something more suitable. He can also stay as long as he wants, though I'm sure he'll require more room eventually."

"What made you tell me this today? You've been thinking about it for a while if you have it planned so thoroughly."

Her cheeks pinked. "I'd been putting it off because I knew you wouldn't want me to leave. Then, this morning I couldn't help but hear . . ." She bobbed her head from side to side.

"Oh," I said softly. "I'm sorry."

"It's not your fault. The door was closed. I just happened to be awake and coming back from jogging in the park. It simply made me realize that I needed to tell you sooner rather than later. The tenant will move out next week, and once she's out, I'll make sure I don't need any renovations before I move in. I don't think it'll take too long. I walked through last week. It's in great shape, and I've already talked to friends about coming over to paint for me. We'll grill, and have a party, and at the end of the evening, everyone can help me move my things inside."

I sighed and gave her a hug. "We never expected you to do this."

"I know, and it's part of why I'm doing it."

I released Jena and grabbed one of Freya's yogurts from the fridge. "I know it's short notice, but would you mind if I took Monday off? William needs to go to Savannah for business, and I'd like to go with him."

"Of course, I don't mind. When will you go?"

"We talked about it this morning and thought that we'd leave tomorrow after lunch. That way, Freya can nap on the trip and not be all fussy in the seat for a long period of time. Monday, he'll take care of whatever it is he has to do. He wants to return after lunch again, but it depends on how much he can get done in the morning. Worst case scenario, we come back Tuesday. He doesn't think it should be necessary, though."

"We can always call you if something comes up," said Jena with a gentle smile. "Don't worry about it."

"Thanks."

She squeezed my hand. "You know I've only ever wanted you happy. I'm glad that all of this has worked out for the best. I didn't want to like William when I met him, but Charlie and I both failed spectacularly at that. We think he's perfect for you—just in case you don't see that yourself."

"I do see it." I watched Freya move a Cheerio around her tray with one finger. "I knew on the island, but with his situation, we couldn't be together then. We've talked a lot since he's been here, and I don't think I would've been happy waiting in the wings for him to get a divorce. Besides, it would've made matters worse for him with his ex-wife." How many nights had we laid in bed discussing all sorts of things—a lot like we had on the island?

"I know you've forgiven him, but does that mean he's forgiven you for not telling him about his daughter?"

I opened my mouth but jumped at the deep voice that came from behind me. "Yes, I have."

Jena flinched. "I'm sorry. It's probably none of my business but—"

"You want to see your sister happy. My father asked me a similar question a week or two ago. I'm not upset. Elle was correct, though. If Elle and I had been together while I was separated from Claire, she would've done everything in her power to ensure the divorce dragged on forever. I needed to be free from Claire first. Even so, she managed to prolong the proceedings so they only ended about seven months ago." William kissed Freya on top of the head and put his arm around me.

My sister held out her hand to him. "For what it's worth, I want both of you to be happy."

He smiled and took the olive branch she offered. "We will be. I know we will be."

Chapter 20

I sat with Freya while we waited for William. He and his father managed to take care of most of the paperwork on Sunday after we'd arrived, so after a quick trip to his office on Monday morning, we met a realtor at his beautifully restored home in the historic district. I couldn't believe he was selling it to move into the much smaller upstairs living area with me, but he assured me several times that he preferred to be in Marysville with us to living in the home he'd once shared with his ex-wife. After such a confession, I could only help him label certain pieces of furniture to be moved so we could use them or put them into storage. The rest he wished to sell.

One of the best things about the trip had been his excitement to show me the places he adored: the tree he used to climb in his parents' backyard, where he went to high school, and lastly, his favorite restaurant, which was where we decided to have lunch on Monday before we returned to Marysville.

When I glanced up from answering a text from Charlie, William was weaving his way through the tables from the restrooms. He took the seat across from me while our daughter sat perched in a high chair eating her toddler snacks. We'd already ordered, and the waiter stopped to drop our drinks off before he moved on to the next table.

William grinned widely. "Do you want to do anything special before we drive back?"

"Only if you have something else you want to show me. I don't think it'll take long for Freya to fall asleep. She's had a busy morning."

He bussed our daughter's cheek with his finger. "Good point. She does look tired. We'll grab our luggage from my dad's and head back after we eat."

"You don't have anything else you need to do?" When he'd mentioned driving to Savannah, I'd assumed he'd had more planned than this.

"No, most of it was the stack of papers I went through with Dad last night while you gave Freya a bath. My assistant now has everything she needs to run the office here and Dad will remain for another few weeks in the event she has any problems.

"I can't believe he found a house in Marysville already."

William laughed and nodded his head. "It was definitely a surprise. With Addy's husband being from Charleston, Addy won't have to split her time as much to see him when she visits, and since I'll be living in Marysville with you as well, it makes sense for him to move closer."

"It does. Otherwise, he'd be here all by himself."

William put his hand over mine where it rested on the table. "We haven't talked about Jena moving. Are you upset she's leaving?"

I gave a one-shouldered shrug. "I suppose I am a little, even though she's only moving out to the garage apartment. I just don't want her to feel like she has to—like we've crowded her out."

He trailed his fingers across the back of my hand, making me relax a little since he asked the question. "I honestly don't think she feels that way," he said. "She seems happy for us."

"She is. She's even told me she is."

"Then don't continue to stress over it. I don't know if you've noticed, but she's gone out to dinner a few times by herself in the last few weeks. Personally, I think she's been dating someone on the sly."

I inhaled sharply and my eyes bulged. "She's always told me when she goes out with a guy. Why would she suddenly keep it a secret?"

He shook his head. "I don't know. Maybe she wants to keep things to herself for now." He put his forearms on the table and leaned forward. "It would also explain why she wants to move into the garage apartment. We would get our privacy. She would get her own too."

Bits and pieces of the last month came back to me: Jena going for walks after work or to dinner on her own, going to the movies once on a Sunday afternoon all by herself, and that one morning . . . "Oh my God! She made the walk of shame and Charlie and I missed it!"

William chuckled and furrowed his brow. "What?"

"Do you remember when she said she was meeting a friend for a few drinks a week ago?" He nodded and his eyebrows dipped down in the middle. "We stayed up to watch the rest of that movie, but she never turned up. When I got up the next morning for work, I heard her come in the door to the balcony. I thought she'd gone for an early run, but I just realized that I never woke up when she came in the night before. I always wake up. She made the walk of shame and Charlie and I never got to tease her about it."

The waiter placed our food in front of us and the topic changed while we ate. The food was excellent but what I enjoyed most was merely sitting with William and experiencing something he loved.

Once he paid the check, he picked up Freya and we walked outside, making our way down the sidewalk to the car. As we turned the corner, I nearly bowled someone over.

"Oh! I'm so sorry."

When I stepped back, the woman looked to William and one of her nostrils lifted like she was about to snarl. "William, how are you?" Her tone wasn't friendly, not friendly at all.

I glanced between them, but it wasn't until I looked back at the woman that I really noticed the man beside her. How? Why? Every muscle in my body tightened, and I suddenly had a niggling feeling who the woman I almost toppled over was, even without the introduction. I gripped William's hand and held on tight.

"Hello, Claire," said William. "If you'll excuse us."

"Aren't you going to introduce me?" she asked with an extra-large helping of sarcasm.

"No, I'm not. Goodbye.

I peeked back over my shoulder as he pulled me away. His ex-wife and the man accompanying her both watched us, but by the time we reached the car, they'd disappeared. It was ridiculous, but I couldn't stop shaking. I'd been so, so stupid.

William strapped our daughter into her car seat while I climbed into the passenger side and buckled up. When he pulled away from the curb, he took my hand. "I'm sorry about that." A tear fell to my cheek and made a warm path down my face. "Elle, are you okay?"

I shook my head and sobbed. "I'm sorry."

His eyes kept shifting back and forth between me and the road. "Honey, you're scaring me."

I waved my hands and shook my head. He needed to concentrate on driving and not me. "We'll talk when we get to your dad's." I also couldn't have him turning around to beat the crap out of whoever it was. I still couldn't believe it.

When we pulled into the driveway at his dad's, William took Freya out of her seat and followed me inside. Once he set her on the floor with a few toys, he took me in his arms and rubbed my back. "What is it? What has you so upset? Is it Claire? Don't let her bother you. She's not worth it."

"I don't understand." I heaved and swallowed. "How? I'm so stupid. I didn't even consider . . ."

"You're the last person I'd call stupid, Elle. Please, just tell me what's going on?"

I drew back from him and held out my arm, pointing in no direction in particular. "That man with your ex-wife. He's the one from the park. The one who told me the sob story that you'd fired him and what a wonderful human being your wife was."

His eyebrows shot up to nearly his hairline and he gave an incredulous guffaw. "You have got to be kidding me."

"I don't understand who he is! And how did he know about me? Because the whole thing really has me kind of freaked out." The trembling hadn't stopped and I crossed my arms over my chest.

"I didn't expect the two of you back so soon." Mr. Davies looked between the two of us. "What's going on?"

"Elle knows who the man is that warned her off of me."

"Really?" said Mr. Davies, the pitch of his voice higher than usual. "Who was he?"

"Claire's lover, Jeremiah Hunter."

I tightened my arms around myself. "But, how did he know? How did he discover where to find me?"

William groaned and rubbed his face with his hands. "I know how. I'm so sorry. That's my fault."

Why was he sorry? Did he tell that woman about me when he returned? No, he couldn't have or he would've mentioned it to me. What did that mean? "I don't understand."

"When I first returned from the island, I told Claire to move out, but she refused. Rather than argue, I moved in with my father and started the divorce proceedings. The house was mine before the marriage and part of the agreement, so I decided to let my lawyer handle that. One evening, Dad went out with some friends to watch a football game, and I stayed behind. I was tired and wanted to go to bed." He stared at the floor as he spoke. "When I got out of the shower, Claire was in my room. She wore this ludicrous negligee. It didn't occur to me at the time, but now that I think about it, she kept stuttering and looking everywhere but at me. I'd left my laptop open because it had frozen. I'd hoped that while I showered the issue would resolve itself so I wouldn't have to restart it, but it hadn't gone to sleep when I came back."

His father pointed at him. "I remember that. She'd found the key to the back door and used it to get in. You had to call the police to make her leave."

"I did. I think it was an attempt to get me back, but when I asked for a divorce, she did accuse me of cheating on her. At the time, I was certain she was grasping for straws. She had no way of knowing what happened on the island."

"She had no clue." His father gave a rueful chuckle. "I'd bet anything she saw an opportunity to snoop into your finances with your laptop open, and instead, she noticed the photo on your screen and got distracted."

"You had a photo of me as your wallpaper?" Freya let out a string of babbles and grabbed my leg, pulling herself up. I picked her up and held her on my hip while she laid her head on my shoulder. "She saw my photo on your computer and decided to send that man to lie to me?"

"She couldn't prove we'd had an affair, which was what she'd need for the divorce, so instead, she must've decided to screw with you. I had your name and phone number written down. It wouldn't take much to figure out where you lived and watch you."

I swallowed whatever burned the base of my throat. "So, she sent her boyfriend to do her dirty work."

"She knew she wasn't getting any of my son's money," said his father, "so she decided he couldn't have what he wanted so desperately."

"I feel so foolish. I let what he said convince me that I shouldn't call you and tell you about Freya." I frowned. "There's no way he missed that I was pregnant. I'm surprised they didn't try to prove we had an affair because of that."

"Then she'd be splitting the money she so desperately wanted with my child."

His father sat in his favorite chair. "She'd never accept that. She made it perfectly clear what she was contesting about the divorce."

I cuddled Freya closer. "What if they've been watching me ever since?"

"You said you'd only seen him the one time," said William. "He probably thought he'd achieved what he'd set out to do and never bothered after. I wonder if she promised him money if she managed to get a bigger settlement from me."

"I'm so sorry." My voice was faint. I wanted to crawl in a hole and hide while I cried my eyes out. How did people like that exist? "It never occurred to me that he was . . ."

William strode over and wrapped me in his arms again. "Why would you? You had no reason to know he was connected to Claire. He didn't lie about me firing him. He did work for me, and my dad did hire him, but when equipment came up missing from one of the worksites, I set up cameras around the property. I caught him stealing. That's why I terminated his employment. I didn't realize until after I returned from the island that he'd been the man screwing my wife too."

He kissed me on my hair and kissed Freya's head. "We've put all of that behind us, and I want to keep it there where it belongs. I don't want you blaming yourself for this. Don't let this put a damper on how happy we've been. I want nothing more than to move ahead with you and not look back."

"As lovely as that is, Son," said his dad, drawing our attention. "I'm hiring an investigator to keep an eye on both of them for a while. I want to make sure they aren't still following Ellie or my granddaughter. One or both of them had to watch her in order to know her habits to begin with."

"I suppose that's a good idea." William's heavy sigh caressed my temple. "I don't want to take any chances. I also don't want to get mired down in the past. We're moving forward, and I want to live for the present and what we have, not what Claire and that man took away from us. They've stolen enough of our time and our lives."

He was right. I didn't want any of this to put a damper on our weekend or influence the choices we'd made for our future. We just needed one thing. "William?"

"Yes, love?"

"Take us home."

His dimples peeked from his cheeks as he grinned. "That sounds perfect."

Chapter 20

Two weeks later, Jena had her big apartment move-in bash. Everyone we knew came, including my and William's fathers. Micah even showed and chipped in on the painting before he insisted on taking a few family pictures of me, William, and Freya. We'd had too many people for the tiny living space, so Jena shooed us out to get dressed so we could pose with the pumpkins and the potted mums on the back patio. It was fall, the back yard looked amazing, and Micah didn't want to waste a perfectly beautiful day.

"Those were fun, y'all," he said with his heavy drawl as he put down his camera. "It doesn't surprise me that you'd be photogenic, William. The camera loves Ellie and your daughter, so I would expect you to have excellent genes too."

Luckily, William laughed off Micah's comment while I walked over to hug my long-time friend. "Thank you."

"Of course, sweetie. I can't believe your luck, though. He's cute. Are you sure he's not gay?"

I bit my bottom lip instead of bursting into gales of laughter. "I'm positive."

"Darn." Micah sighed dramatically. He gave William an up and down glance. "If you find out he is, sweetheart, hook me up, will you?"

I kissed his cheek. "Definitely." Micah always had a bit of a flamboyant silly streak. One thing I did know for sure was that William was one-hundred percent into women—me in particular—and he had no plans or eyes for anyone else.

While Micah packed up his camera equipment, I watched Jena standing on the patio of her new place speaking to Connor Willoughby, the real estate agent who found our office and living space. Something about the tilt of her head and the way she looked at him had me raising my eyebrows. More than friendship existed between them. She peered at Connor from under her eyelashes, confirming my suspicions. Question was: why was she being so sneaky about it?

Since Savannah, I'd been positive about her being involved with someone, but I'd never questioned her about it. Maybe today would be the day?

"What does that expression mean?" I jumped at William's voice right next to my ear.

"Just noticing something."

"She's flirting with him." He put his arm around me. "It's subtle. If I didn't know Jena, I probably wouldn't see it." He was right. I hadn't seen them together since we viewed the house. It was no wonder I'd missed this.

"I'm going to go change Freya back into her play clothes," said William. "Otherwise, she'll ruin this dress." As I glanced in William's direction, I caught sight of Charlie's brother, Brandon, as he paused mid-step in his walk up the driveway.

"Definitely," I replied while keeping watch on Brandon as his jaw tightened and released.

"We'll be right back. Be good."

I didn't glance at William as he carried our daughter away but his voice moved while he spoke. I was certain he'd called the last over his shoulder. I put up a hand, waving behind me. "Uh, huh." I was too busy gawking at what I'd neglected to notice for how long? Where had I been when all this happened?

Brandon stood in the center of the driveway, rigid, his arms limp by his sides as he looked away from my sister for no more than a moment. Brandon and Jena had been best friends for as long as I could remember, but how did I not see this? Since when had he been in love with her?

In all the years they'd been inseparable, Jena had never considered Brandon more than a friend. Poor guy! He was stuck in the friend zone, which had to be the worst seats in the house at times like these.

William passed Charlie on the way up the balcony steps and I waved her over. "Did you know about this?"

Charlie glanced back and forth between Jena and Brandon for a moment. "Which part?" She bit her lip and peered at me out of the corner of her eye.

I inhaled sharply and coughed, choking on my own spit. "You knew!" I whispered loudly, pointing at her and wagging my finger. "You knew and you didn't tell me. I can't believe the two of you are keeping secrets from me."

"It's not like that, Ellie." She pulled me over and aimed her finger at my chest as though she were scolding me like an errant child. "Brandon confided in me ages ago. I love you, but you know damn well I couldn't divulge what's in his heart. I can't even tell Jena even though I've wanted to beat that girl over the head with it so often I'm surprised I haven't done it yet." I took a peek at Jena. Fortunately, Charlie had moderated her volume, so my sister remained blissfully unaware of our conversation. Charlie happened to look over as Brandon sucked up his pride, walked up to Jena, and kissed her on the cheek. They said a few words before he ducked inside, leaving her to Connor.

After a sigh, Charlie shook her head and started jabbing that finger again. "As for the situation with Connor, you've had enough to deal with between William returning and the two of you becoming a couple again. Jena didn't want to distract you from that."

"She wouldn't distract me. I don't want her hiding things from me because she thinks I'm some fragile creature who can't handle it."

Charlie held out both hands, palms forward. "We never said you couldn't handle it. Jena made the call because she wanted you to enjoy your relationship with William. Now that you know, I'm sure she won't keep things so hush-hush."

"She should know by now that if she's happy, I'm thrilled for her. I'm also sorry. You're right, I wouldn't expect you to break Brandon's confidence. I just don't understand how I've apparently been blind for so long."

Charlie sighed and shrugged. "He's become *very* good at hiding his feelings. One day he'll either give up or she'll finally see him—really see him. If she does, she better not break his heart. I don't want to have to kick her scrawny ass."

"You know she'd never hurt him on purpose." Jena would never intentionally trample on anyone's heart. Unfortunately, that meant they usually flattened hers.

"I know, but I still worry," said Charlie, yanking me toward Jena's apartment. As we approached, Jena stopped speaking and lightly touched Connor's arm. He gave us a polite smile before disappearing inside.

"Ellie's figured you and Connor out," said Charlie. "She isn't too thrilled to have been kept in the dark."

"You could've told me." I didn't speak loudly, choosing instead to put my hands on my hips.

Jena grabbed my hands and squeezed them comfortingly. "I thought it was better this way. We'd dated a little before William returned but nothing serious until after."

"But, you made the walk of shame, and Charlie and I didn't even get to rag you about it!"

A snicker came from Charlie who still lingered at my side. "I definitely let her have it for you."

Jena's face turned several shades of red. "I can't believe you figured that out."

I lifted one eyebrow, and pulling my hands from hers, crossed my arms over my chest. "I figured it out after you told me you wanted to move out here. I hadn't considered the possibility before that moment. I just wish you'd felt like you could share it with me."

"I'm sorry," said Jena. "I promise not to do it again. Please understand that I wanted to help."

"I know you did." My body sagged before I gave in and hugged her. It was impossible to stay mad at her. "And I love you for caring so much, but William and I are in a good place and that's not going to change. It's not like I'm going to lose you because you're dating someone."

"I know. I hope you'll forgive me."

I released her and nodded. "You know I do."

Charlie clapped her hands together while her gaze shifted from Jena to me and back. "Okay, now that we've ironed that out and we're all on the same page can we get down to finishing up the painting and moving so we can have a party. I have wood for the fire pit, and I've got drinks and ice in the coolers on the patio."

"Ellie!" We turned to find Mr. Davies and Addy walking up the drive. "William said you were having a get-together today. We thought we'd come by and see if you need any more help."

"Oh, I can't have you painting." Jena's head shook madly.

"I have an idea." I hugged Mr. Davies and Addy quickly in greeting. "Why don't they help William and me move your furniture down. Then, we can start moving what I have in storage up to replace it as well as what's yours to the patio."

"Jena, darling." Micah sashayed through the front door. "You know everyone is about done with the first coat. They plan on taking a break before putting on a second. With all the fans you've got running, everything should be dry pretty quickly. We can move all your furniture in once it's dry to the touch. We'll just need to leave everything open until you go to bed tonight."

I waved to them both. "We'll go get started upstairs."

"Thank you!" called Jena as I led Mr. Davies and Addy up the stairs.

William opened the door as I climbed the last step, his eyes widening a bit when he saw his sister. "Addy!"

"Hey, Will."

I moved out of the way so William could embrace his sister. Freya leaned her head on her daddy's shoulder and frowned.

"This must be my niece." Addy tweaked Freya's foot, but the little imp wasn't having it. She clung in an impossible grip around William's neck while he laughed and brushed a light kiss to her head.

"It's okay, sweet pea. This is your Aunt Addy."

"Don't worry." His sister waved off our finicky daughter's less than enthusiastic response. "She doesn't know me, but I hope to change that."

I gestured toward the door. "Why don't we sit in the living room and talk. Jena's not in any rush and Freya might be more willing to play with Addy."

"That's a good idea," said Mr. Davies. "I have something I want to discuss with you two, if that's okay."

When we were all in the living room and seated, William's father leaned forward and put his elbows on his knees. "I heard from the investigator I hired to watch Claire and Jeremiah Hunter, though he did a bit more than keep an eye on them."

William's forehead scrunched while he placed a squirming Freya on the floor. "What do you mean?"

"The investigator also checked into her bank records and called in some favors," said Mr. Davies. "He was the same guy I used to follow her two years ago. When I told him about you bumping into Claire, and Ellie's first meeting with Jeremiah Hunter, he became suspicious as well. The coincidence of Hunter showing up in Marysville and happening upon Ellie, in particular, had him concerned. Fortunately, it didn't take him long to discover that Claire has squandered every last cent she received in your financial arrangement. Her car has been repossessed, the townhouse is not far from foreclosure, and Hunter is probably riding the money until there's none left. I imagine he'll bail on Claire once she's penniless."

William rolled his eyes. "He was always an opportunist."

"And he hasn't changed," said Addy. "I couldn't believe it when Dad told me about what he'd done."

"Yes, well." His father wore a peculiar smile. "I'm not sure if Claire knows, but Hunter has several women he's taking for a ride. The investigator found one woman who recently came into money with the death of her husband and another who appears to have very little to her name. He believes Hunter fleeces what he can and feeds it to this other woman—that she's either his partner or someone whom he actually loves."

"Is this Hunter still coming around Marysville?" I bit my lip. A part of me had become more observant of who was around me when I walked in the park or to the supermarket. William and I always ran errands together since our trip to Savannah—even if it was just to the market. I never saw Jeremiah Hunter or Claire, but regardless of how much we wanted to pretend they'd never watched me, they had. They had to have, and this proved that we didn't just accidentally bump into each other twice. We couldn't bury our heads in the sand when we weren't sure of their current intentions.

Mr. Davies shook his head. "Neither of them has left Savannah in the last few weeks. My investigator trailed Hunter while his assistant trailed Claire. He's not only turned over all of the information on Jeremiah Hunter to the police, but also plans on watching them for another couple of weeks to be on the safe side. He thinks they merely wanted to toy with you, Ellie. No proof existed of any relationship between you and my son from your vacation. If you'd confessed to a relationship, they might've tried to pull you into the divorce proceedings, but you said nothing that Claire could use in court. She had no definite proof. Ensuring the two of you remained separated was likely Hunter's idea for revenge on William."

I released a big exhale and relaxed. I hadn't wanted to be so frightened of those people yet I couldn't help but worry about what they were up to and what they were doing. William nodded and squeezed my hand. He'd put on a brave face but he'd confessed to being concerned as well.

Freya took a book from her toys and brought it to her grandfather. With a large grin, he set her in his lap and started to turn the pages while she watched.

Addy lifted her eyebrows at her brother with a giggle. "Freya is adorable, but I can't decide who she resembles more."

"I think she favors William," I said.

William shook his head with a soft smile. "She has my eyes but the rest is all you—particularly when she stubbornly sets her little jaw."

I feigned a gasp. "And you aren't hardheaded? Please."

His low laugh melted my insides and I had to look away before I embarrassed myself; however, when I turned, Addy watched us with a wide grin.

I stood and turned around to William. "I told Jena we'd start moving her belongings down to the patio so when the paint's dry, they simply have to move them inside. Then, we can move what I have in storage up and leave room for what we saved from your house."

"They packed it up yesterday," said Mr. Davies. "I believe the movers said they would make the delivery this afternoon?"

"They'd told me tomorrow when I spoke to them last week." William shrugged. "Either works, especially if we move Jena's furniture out now. Ellie doesn't have much downstairs to carry up here."

"My apartment was rather tiny, and William had a few beautiful antiques that he said came from his mother. We'll have plenty of room for them."

His father nodded. "Yes, he and Addy each have certain pieces she wanted them to have."

Addy stood and brushed her hands on her legs. "What do you want me to do?"

I shook my head and pointed to my daughter, who stood at Addy's feet holding a book up to her. "How about get acquainted with your niece?"

Addy's face lit with a smile. "Do you want me to read that to you?" She sat in one of the chairs and cuddled Freya in her lap.

William pointed to the modern IKEA entertainment center. "I believe everything on that belongs to Jena. Is that right?"

"Yes, she's boxed up the knickknacks and her movies. We'll carry down the television and her Blu-ray player."

After removing the electronics, they moved one piece at a time while I carried down the Blu-ray and its accessories. When I returned, voices from Freya's room led me to the door. Addy and Freya sat on the floor, playing with the toys they'd spread around them.

"I didn't think it would take long for her to warm up to Addy." I glanced over my shoulder at William. His warm breath tickled that sensitive spot just below my ear, making me have to restrain a shiver.

"I simply wanted to make sure she was okay," I said. "I didn't want Addy to struggle if Freya was resistant."

He pointed back at the living room with his thumb. "Coffee table and end tables go down, right?"

"Yes. If you give me a minute, I'll help."

He gave me a smacking kiss on the lips. "Dad and I can do it."

With Addy keeping Freya busy, moving Jena's belongings downstairs took no time at all. I only had a few items in storage, mainly the love seat that matched my sofa and a couple of lamps. Jena had a few items that William and Mr. Davies carried to the driveway, which left the storage room empty. We then gave it a thorough cleaning so when William's office furniture was delivered, we could move it right in.

The moving company showed up after lunch just as Mr. Davies said they would and hauled in what we'd decided to keep from William's Savannah home, including his boxes of belongings and the furniture, which took no time at all to pile into rooms Freya didn't have access to. We didn't want her hurt by an unstable pile falling on her.

When the last of the boxes joined William's bedroom suite in Jena's old room, which was now the guest room, we started prepping food to grill outside. I'd just finished making the potato salad when William strode in the balcony doors.

"With all the fans, the paint is dry to the touch and they're moving the furniture in."

I lifted my eyebrows. They were definitely rushing things. "I hope they don't bump the wall. It's still not completely cured."

He laughed. "Micah is bellowing out orders while Jena is telling people where to put everything. It's really pretty funny."

"I've seen him in bossy diva mode," I said with a chuckle. "I'm not going out there or he'll rope me into working."

Addy laughed while she made a green salad. "I have a friend who is very similar at the conservatory. He's such a sweetheart and will do anything for me."

I nodded while I put the bowl of potato salad in the fridge to keep it cold. "That's Micah. I don't think I've ever had to pay for a photo of Freya. He brings his camera whenever he thinks she needs new portraits and does everything. I've tried to pay him, but he won't take it."

Addy paused in peeling a cucumber. "But you send him work, don't you?"

"Yes, but I still don't expect him to take photos of us for free."

Mr. Davies returned through the balcony doors with several bags in his hand. "I've got beer, wine, and a few bottles of prosecco in the event someone feels like celebrating." He set his groceries on the counter. "One of the bottles is cold. I thought we'd open it before the real party gets started."

William pulled the bottles and either set them in the wine rack or put them in the chiller until he reached one that he set on the counter. "Shall we?"

"Definitely," said his dad. Four glasses were set on the counter, and once William had filled each of them, his father handed us all a bubbly glass. "The Davies family has certainly had its ups and downs. I remember how dejected William appeared when he came home from the island two years ago. At the time, I had to have faith that it would all work out for the best. I hoped and prayed he would find happiness again.

Little did I know when I walked into the office downstairs with Addy, what I set in motion."

William put his arm around me, and I shifted closer to him, wrapping my arm around his back and absorbing some of his strength.

His dad continued, "I'm pleased to welcome Ellie and Freya into the family. It may not be official yet, but to be perfectly honest, I don't think it'll be long before it is."

My face warmed while Addy laughed beside me. After the island, I never expected William's family to welcome me with open arms but they did, unreservedly. Freya and I were so fortunate. They could have held a colossal grudge and I couldn't have blamed them in the least.

"So, I'd like to officially toast their entry to the Davies' family." He held up his glass. "Ellie, Freya, and William."

"To us," we laughed, clinking glasses.

William's father took a tiny sip and looked directly at me. "Now, Ellie, you've insisted on calling me Mr. Davies, but I do hope you'll call me either Dad or Grant in the future."

I crinkled my nose as the bubbles tickled my lip, making William dab my face with a towel while his shoulders shook. "I'll give it a shot," I said.

His father gave a quick nod. "Good."

"Hello in there!" We all turned to Charlie peeking through one of the balcony doors. "Is the food ready to go? Connor's firing up the grill."

"Yes," I said. I picked up the tray of vegetables and meat and handed it over to Charlie. "There's the first batch. Let me know when you're ready for the next. I'll send it out."

Charlie looked over the food with a grin. "Awesome. You're joining us soon, aren't you?"

"We'll be down in a bit. Freya's still sleeping. Her Aunt Addy really wore her out."

Grant picked up a cooler with more drinks. "I'll bring this out to the balcony. I don't want it to leak or sweat on the wood floor."

"I'm going to go peek in on Freya," said William, giving me a peck on the cheek.

"Don't wake her."

He rolled his eyes. "I know."

When I was left with Addy, I sat on one of the barstools and took another sip of my wine to boost my courage. "I hope we can be friends. I never meant to hurt William. I hope you know that."

She nodded. "I know. Just like I know he never meant to hurt you—even though he was wrong. Everything is as it should be now. I think we should move forward and not concentrate on the hurt of the past, don't you?"

"I do. It's what William and I have worked so hard to accomplish not only for us but also for the sake of our daughter."

Addy grinned. "Good! I've always wanted a sister."

"Well, you may as well count Jena and Charlie too. We sort of come as a package deal."

Addy plopped down on the stool next to me and tapped her glass to mine. "Sounds perfect."

"What sounds perfect?" That deep voice that meant home, family, love—that meant everything—resonated through the room.

I looked up at William with a grin I couldn't hold in. "Me, I'm perfect."

He dropped down onto the stool next to me while he chuckled warmly. "I suppose you are."

"I am?" The surprise in my voice rendering the tone a bit higher than usual. But still, what did he mean by that?

"Yes," he said, nodding. "Because you are nothing less than perfect for me."

Chapter 21

June (8 months later)

The music changed and I snapped to attention, checking each and every bridesmaid in front of me until Jena pushed me into the line.

"You're not working today, remember? Now, you know how to hold those flowers. And whatever you do, don't trip."

"No pressure," I said, laughing and stepping forward as a bridesmaid decked in a flowing dress slipped through the doors.

"Don't forget to make—"

I rolled my eyes. "To make sure Freya sees me so she'll walk down the aisle. I know. You've told me a million times." Yes, my voice revealed my exasperation with my sister. I couldn't help it! I'd organized the wedding. I knew more than anyone what needed to be done. I also wanted it to be picture perfect.

The next bridesmaid in line started her processional, and I approached the double doors at the back of St. Michael's.

Jena leaned closer while I waited for my cue. "Micah gave me a glimpse of the photos. The shots he took of Addy by the wrought iron gates. Absolutely gorgeous!"

"Aren't they?" My voice was definitely more than a little gushy. My stomach rolled and I swallowed hard. Not now!

"Are you okay?" Jena's brows drew down in the middle as she frowned. "You're looking a little pale all of a sudden. You aren't nervous, are you?"

"I'm fine." The doors opened in front of me, so I drew my shoulders back, took a deep breath, and started my procession down the aisle. When I reached the flower-decked altar, I shifted to the side and pivoted so I faced the rear of the chapel while I waited for the matron of honor to join me. Once she'd made her way beside me, the rear doors opened and Charlie led Freya to the back of the aisle. She set my daughter on the floor, handed her an ornately frilled basket of rose petals, and scattered a few to the floor. Freya had a field day at the rehearsal with the silk ones we'd used. Hopefully, the two hundred and fifty guests today wouldn't deter her excitement.

Only, Freya peered around at the congregation with wide eyes while the doors shut behind her. She appeared so little standing there all by herself. I shifted forward and waved. I pretended to drop rose petals, but she only stood there frozen and staring. The next thing I knew, in a flurry of tulle, she ran from the back of the church straight into my arms while the guests all chuckled.

I carried her back down a portion of the aisle and helped her strew a few blush-colored rose petals before we returned to the side of the altar with the remainder of the bridesmaids. How Freya's little feet didn't trip on all the puffy tulle of her flower girl dress was beyond me! I glanced over to William, who stood with the groomsmen. He wore a grin the size of Texas on his face. How he loved his little girl!

Finally, the double doors opened to reveal Addy perfectly framed by the arched doorframe. William's sister exuded happiness and was so radiant I doubt anyone noticed her father at her side. She certainly outshined everyone in the room, but she was supposed to. She was the bride. It was her day.

Her low-backed romantic gown suited her personality and the string quartet of her friends playing the processional made the ceremony one of the most beautiful weddings I'd ever arranged. We rarely had the selection of musicians and music as we did for today.

I choked back tears as the couple exchanged their heartfelt vows as well as the rings. I'd gotten to know Addy's fiancé over the past eight months. Ben was a genuinely nice guy and adored Addy to bits, which was all that mattered to William and me.

William cocked an eyebrow at me during the vows, and I tilted my head. What did he mean by that expression? Before I could think about it too much, Freya spotted her father and escaped my hand, running behind Addy and Ben to him. "Daddy!"

Without a pause, he scooped her up and put her on his hip. She'd certainly become daddy's little girl, not that he'd ever voiced one complaint. She'd follow him everywhere if he let her—and I mean everywhere. I loved the two of them so much I thought my heart would overflow, I felt so much. I was so fortunate that William forgave me—that we forgave one another.

I dabbed the corner of my eye with my finger and his dimples deepened. I couldn't cry! If even one tear hit my cheek, he'd win the stupid bet we'd made this morning. I couldn't have that! I blinked quickly and stared straight at him. *I* certainly wasn't crying.

After Addy kissed her new husband and he led her down the aisle, I stepped forward until I took William's free arm for the walk out of the church. Freya rested her head on his shoulder, hiding her face in his neck.

"Was that a tear?" he whispered.

"No, I had something in my eye."

"Uh huh." He kissed my hairline his lips smiling against my temple. "I'll be collecting on that bet later, sweetheart. By the way, have I told you yet that you look amazing? That color is beautiful on you."

Addy did have lovely understated taste. Our blush gowns coordinated with the roses and the flowers in the bouquets and helped accentuate the romantic atmosphere she desired. I couldn't wait to add some of the photos to our portfolio.

When we reached the limo, we piled inside and waited for Grant so we could drive to Marysville for the reception. Addy's new in-laws had insisted on having the celebration at their house, but when William bought the sizeable red brick antebellum home that went up for sale next door to where we were living, Addy changed her mind quickly—particularly once William had the trim painted and the landscaping completely overhauled.

The backyard was also one of the largest in the middle of town and perfect for entertaining. We installed a beautiful wrought iron gate to connect our property to the backyard of the office, which made even more room for the reception. A dance floor would be erected on our lawn and the patio in the backyard of the office would be used for dinner, a bar, and extra seating.

"Are you alright?" William glanced back as he buckled in Freya. "You looked white as a sheet when you walked down the aisle."

"I'm fine." I kept my tone light. The last thing I wanted was another lecture on seeing the doctor.

"If you still have that stomach bug, you should go to the doctor. A virus doesn't linger for three weeks."

"I'm fine." The raised eyebrows he gave me proved he didn't believe a word coming out of my mouth. Oh well! So what if I was tired all of the time and my stomach didn't like me these days.

Grant hopped in. "Are we ready?"

Once he closed the door, the limo pulled away from the curb for the short drive to Marysville. When we arrived, Addy and her new husband stood in the receiving line, greeting their guests, so William and I settled Freya with some lunch and put her down for a nap.

As William snuck out of her room, he crossed his fingers, the baby monitor held up in the other hand. "Are you ready to enjoy ourselves for a while?" We walked through the French doors in the living room to the party going on in our backyard. A band played upbeat music, waiters milled around with glasses of Champagne on gleaming silver trays, and Addy stood to one corner of the dance floor chatting animatedly with her friends. She was happier than I'd ever seen her, but that was how it was supposed to be, wasn't it? I wasn't unhappy although I definitely wanted that feeling of euphoria and absolute bliss that came with committing to someone for the rest of our lives.

"What are you thinking?" His warm breath tickled my ear.

"That she looks overjoyed." I leaned against him and sighed. I knew one day William and I would take that step but he simply hadn't asked yet. He'd moved out of the room we'd let him use as an office and into his own building a few doors down. He'd also bought a house for the three of us—for our fledgling family. I'd have loved to contribute to buying our home, but of course, he hadn't told me until the sale was a done deal. Instead, he surprised me with it on my birthday. He could be such a dear. We'd just been so busy. Even if he'd asked, I don't know when we would've married.

"Let's get a drink." He laced his fingers with mine and led me to the bar. "Two glasses of the red please."

"I'll have mineral water instead, please."

He frowned and squeezed my hand. "You're going to the doctor first thing Monday morning. I want to make sure this isn't something serious."

"I'm fine."

"You keep saying that, but I don't believe you."

I huffed and leaned against him as the girl behind the bar handed us our drinks. I was fine. He'd been so overprotective since I had that bout of pneumonia a month ago. I know it scared him, but I'd recovered. I didn't need him to be such a mother hen.

We talked to guests and milled around until the luncheon was served and we all ate. After Addy danced the first with her father and her husband and everyone joined them on the dance floor, William whispered, "Dance with me." His voice had that low tone that made me squeeze my thighs together tight and my breath catch in the back of my throat. I crumbled, letting him tug me to the center of the dancers and wrap his arms around me while he swayed me around the parquet floor. I closed my eyes and let him lead, enjoying the feel of his solid muscles beneath his shirt and the scent of his cologne. I didn't want to be anywhere else.

Once Freya woke up, my dad and Grant helped keep her busy, allowing us to have more time to dance and simply be together. Between our fathers, Jena, and Charlie, Freya was kept well entertained until she fell asleep two hours before her bedtime while sitting in William's lap, and we put her to bed.

After the fireworks and after Addy and Ben charged through a shower of birdseed to depart for their honeymoon, my father and Grant left to their own homes, leaving us to enjoy the warm night and the star-laden sky.

"Why don't we sit on the balcony?" William had that look in his eye. If there hadn't been a crew cleaning the mess from the reception, I would've thought he had something hot and sweaty on his mind but William would never take a chance like that with so many people close by.

Instead, we sat in our favorite double rocker and he wrapped his arm around me. "You did a fantastic job on Addy's wedding."

"Thank you. I just wish your father would've taken it as a gift rather than sneaking off and paying Charlie behind my back."

That deep laugh made my insides flutter, just like it had on the island almost three years ago. "He knew she wouldn't refuse the money."

"No, Charlie is the consummate businesswoman. She'll never turn down a paycheck."

He took a deep breath and nuzzled his nose against my hair. "Have you given any thought to planning one of these for us?" My head jerked up and his smiling eyes caught mine. "Maybe not so grand. I don't mind if you want it, but I'd rather have something more intimate."

"Is that a proposal, Mr. Davies?" I arched one eyebrow.

"It can be, Miss Barret." He watched me for a moment before he rolled his eyes. "You're going to make me ask, aren't you?"

"If you want an answer."

He stood, dropped to one knee, and took my hand. "Elle, I knew when you first offered to share your table with me that you'd change my life. Little did I realize how much. Since that evening, my life has been transformed into what I'd always dreamed of having—happiness, a family. You're everything I ever wanted and I thank God every day that he brought you and Freya into my life."

A warm tear dropped to my cheek and I left it alone to form a damp trail to my chin. He brushed it away and ran his knuckles down the side of my neck.

"All I want now is to make it official." He reached into his pocket and pulled out a leather box. "Elle, will you marry me?" He opened the black jewelry case to the most beautiful vintage-looking engagement ring. Tiny round diamonds formed an ornate halo for the brilliant one-carat round-cut diamond in the middle.

I clasped my hands in front of me. "Yes."

His dimples peeked out as he beamed. The ring was removed from its velvet bed and slid onto my finger while I watched. I couldn't believe he'd finally asked. Even though I expected it, I'd still waited and waited. If he'd taken much longer, I would've asked him instead.

The stone reflected the light from the lamps on the porch. "It's perfect."

"It was my mother's. Dad wanted you to have it."

"I'll have to thank him in the morning." I bent over and pressed my lips to his. My heart beat so quickly, it felt like it would come out of my chest.

"Hold on," he said softly. He stood and turned around, cupping his hands around his mouth. "Go!"

"What are you doing?" I laughed at his silliness.

"You'll see." He took the seat next to me and pulled me close, claiming my lips once more. Threading my fingers into the back of his hair, I deepened the kiss as he groaned into my mouth. He'd just cradled my cheek in his palm when a loud boom made me jump. I looked over the trees behind the house to find a rainbow of fireworks bursting into vivid color in the inky-black sky.

"You're crazy." I laughed and shook my head.

"I had the guys save a few for later. I hope you don't mind."

"I doubt anyone missed them earlier." I curled my legs up over his and wrapped my arms around him. "I have a present for you too."

"You do?" He turned to me with both eyebrows raised.

"Yup." I bit my lip while I tried not to grin like an idiot. "What do you think about giving Freya a little brother or sister?"

He gave me a sidelong look. "You know I want more children, but I thought you hoped to wait another year or so."

I shrugged with a smile. "Yeah . . . well, nature had other ideas."

His jaw went slack and his eyes widened to the size of fifty-cent pieces. "I don't understand. How? You take your pill every morning like clockwork."

"Do you remember when I started feeling better after the pneumonia?"

One side of his lips turned up in a wicked grin. "When we christened the antique dining room table? I'll never be able to look at that piece of furniture and not see you naked across the top."

I laughed softly while my cheeks burned. "Anyway, I was still on antibiotics and apparently, they can make the pill ineffective. I think we're doomed to be surprised by our children."

His entire body relaxed as he rested back into the seat. "That's why you've been sick to your stomach so much. You never had a stomach virus."

I shook my head, my lips tugging up on one side. "No, but I did want the perfect moment to tell you. After you proposed, I thought it might make a nice engagement present. Besides, we'll need to get moving on those wedding plans. I'd rather not look like a beached whale in my wedding pictures."

"I've seen your maternity photos from Freya. You never resembled a beached whale. You looked so feminine and beautiful."

"You'll have to remember to tell me that when I get that far along. I won't believe you, but you'll definitely earn brownie points. Who knows how I'll repay you?" His low chuckle and the finger skimming over the column of my neck made me shift in my seat. I wanted him. I also wanted to enjoy this moment. Ignoring that ache he so easily caused, I turned and watched the last of the fireworks fade from the sky. "William?"

"Yes?"

"What do you think of a beach wedding?" My head rested on the back of the swing while my eyes met his.

He smiled so sweetly my heart nearly stopped. "I think it sounds perfect."

The End

Acknowledgements

I adore writing Regency, but every once in a while, I have to clear the palate so to speak with something different. Thanks a ton, to everyone who reads this series! I hope you fall in love with the characters as I have and look forward to the next installment with Jena and the gentleman that ends up winning her heart. Will it be Connor or will Brandon get a chance? I know, but I'm not telling!

For my family, I always give my love and appreciation for their unwavering support. My husband listens to all my frustrations. Poor guy! He helped me out a bunch with this by copyediting it for me. I've tried to enlist him as a proofreader before but the guy doesn't generally read romance. He finally caved and used his wicked grammar skills to help me. By the time this book is released, he should be winging his way back from some work engagement or another. I can't wait for him to get here. I love you, Brandon!

My children have chipped in on one book or another with either proofreading (the less racy books of course!) and sometimes title help and giving my cover a look for any issues. It's amazing to me that they take pride in what I've accomplished. They are always a part of it because I couldn't do this without them!

Huge thanks to everyone from the online forums who have supported me in the past and now.

I've had a number of betas along the way, but Carol S. Bowes has stuck with me from the beginning, or nearly the beginning and was my wonderful editor for this go around. We have become amazing friends, and she is always a willing ear or eyes when I need an opinion on anything from a book to a blog post. I have learned so much from her.

A huge thanks to my friends both in the military community and outside of it. Friends are precious and a good friend, is priceless. I thank my friends for every willing ear and every laugh that's gotten me through a rough day.

JAFF is a relatively small and tight-knit community, and I love that. The support of other authors in the genre is lovely as is the support and devotion of our fan base. Thank you to everyone who has purchased my books, left me wonderful messages, and followed me after reading one of my stories. I wouldn't be able to have this much fun without your support and encouragement.

About the Author

L.L. Diamond is more commonly known as Leslie to her friends and Mom to her three kids. A native of Louisiana, she spent the majority of her life living within an hour of New Orleans before following her husband all over as a military wife. Louisiana, Mississippi, California, Texas, New Mexico, Nebraska, and now England have all been called home along the way.

Aside from mother and writer, Leslie considers herself a perpetual student. She has degrees in biology and studio art but will devour any subject of interest simply for the knowledge. Her most recent endeavors have included certifications to coach swimming, certifying as a fitness instructor and indoor cycling instructor, and is currently studying to be a personal trainer. As an artist, her concentration is in graphic design, but watercolor is her medium of choice with one of her watercolors featured on the cover of her second book, *A Matter of Chance*. She is also a member of the Jane Austen Society of North America. Leslie also plays flute and piano, but much like Pride and Prejudice's Elizabeth Bennet, she is always in need of practice!

Leslie's books include: *Rain and Retribution, A Matter of Chance, An Unwavering Trust, The Earl's Conquest, Particular Intentions, Particular Attachments, Unwrapping Mr. Darcy, It's Always Been You, It's Always Been Us,* and *It's Always Been You and Me.*